I AM NOT
ALONE

I AM NOT ALONE

Francisco X. Stork

SCHOLASTIC PRESS

NEW YORK

Library of Congress Cataloging-in-Publication Data available

ISBN 978-1-338-73626-7

10 9 8 7 6 5 4 3 2 1   23 24 25 26 27

Printed in Italy   183
First edition, July 2023

Book design by Abby Dening

FOR ELLA RUTH KLOOSTERBOER

CHAPTER 1

Time to be free!

Alberto opened his eyes when he heard the voice. He was in bed, the gray light of dawn outside his window. There was no one else in his room.

It was the same voice he had heard a dozen or so times the past month. A man's voice. Not angry. Not loud. Not like when Wayne yelled at him to do something. The voice was insistent, nagging, high-pitched sometimes. Alberto didn't fear what it said or how it sounded as much as the fact that it was there. So real. There was sweat on his temples, on his legs.

The first time Alberto heard the voice he was riding the subway. The voice whispered, *I got you.* Alberto thought there was someone behind him, but there was no one close to him. Sometimes the voice came when he was working and sometimes when he was holding baby Chato. Now here it was again, telling him it was time to be free, whatever that meant. A dream? Lupe had once told him that one day he would even dream in English. Had the six months of evening classes at Brooklyn College finally paid off? But if the voice was a dream, even if it was in English, why was he trembling? The voices in dreams are invisible. This voice shone like a neon light.

Alberto turned on the lamp next to his bed and leaned onto the window ledge. The cold air felt good. All this week he had slept with the window open. The first time he was able to do that since he and his sister Lupe moved into the apartment six months ago in early November right after baby Chato was born. Already there was movement on the streets. Officer Ramos, the policeman who lived in apartment 3D, was walking his dog. A man stepped out of a white van with a stack of newspapers. Alberto suddenly remembered that it was Sunday. He did not work Sundays. Was that what the voice meant? Maybe today he would be free. He could walk to Coney Island if he wanted to. Or maybe go back to the pottery studio and glaze the bowl he had made.

Alberto was startled by another sound, this time coming from Lupe's room. It was a man snoring. Wayne must have come in after Alberto fell asleep. That was not good. The days when Wayne visited Lupe were hard days. There would be fighting. Lupe wanted Wayne to marry her, to be a full-time husband to her and a full-time father to baby Chato. To be a parent was more than providing an apartment and an allowance for food and diapers and doctors. Wayne disagreed. He thought Lupe didn't know how good she had it—a luxury apartment in Flatbush, no financial worries. "I even employ that dumbass brother of yours."

The walls in the apartment were thin. Alberto heard things that were not pleasant. He heard Lupe argue with Wayne about the wages that Wayne paid Alberto. Alberto got seven dollars an hour while Lucas and Jimbo got fifteen. And Alberto was careful when he worked. The tenants praised Alberto's work and sometimes complained about the sloppy work of Lucas and Jimbo.

"You need to pay him what you pay others," Lupe told him.

"Does he pay *me* rent for living here? Does he pay *me* for his food? Room and board, that's why he gets paid less."

There were times when the urge to hit Wayne was so powerful Alberto had to sit on his hands or breathe twenty times or walk around the block. He was bigger and stronger than Wayne. He could pick him up and throw him out the window. Alberto wanted Lupe to leave Wayne. They would find a way to make it on their own. But Lupe needed Wayne. She believed that without Wayne, she would relapse into addiction. And Alberto needed Wayne as well. He gave Alberto work and did not report him to immigration. Half of what Alberto earned he sent to Mexico. His mother, his grandmother, and his two little sisters, Mercedes and Chela, they all lived with the money he sent.

Was it true that he was a dumbass like Wayne said? Three years ago, when they first came to the United States, Lupe tried to enroll him in a public school. Alberto was fifteen. A lady at the school gave him a test, asked him questions in Spanish that made him dizzy. Afterward, the woman told Lupe that Alberto would need to be placed in a special class.

"What is *special*?" he asked Lupe on the way home.

"You would be with other kids that have a hard time learning."

He thought for a while about Lupe's words. Then he said, "I'll find a way to learn English, but I'm not going to a special class. I don't belong in school. Mamá and Papá were okay with that." The director of his school in Ticul had told his mother and father that Alberto had to repeat fourth grade because he was so far behind the other students. That's when Alberto convinced his father to let him work as an apprentice potter.

"I know, I know. But it's different here. Without school you won't get anywhere. You won't be able to get a good job."

"I will learn on my own."

And he had. At least, he was trying. He got a library card and took books out. One at a time. Children's books at first, but the book he was reading now was about Japanese pottery. He was also slowly making his way, a page or two a night, through the high school equivalency workbooks that Lupe got for him. It would take another five years at the rate he was going before he could earn a high school certificate, assuming he could pass all the tests. His mind worked slow, he knew that, but slow was not the same as dumbass.

Baby Chato began to cry. Alberto opened the chest of drawers in his room and took out blue jeans and a T-shirt. He sat on his bed and waited to hear Lupe open the door to her bedroom. He would tell her that she could go back to sleep while he took care of the baby.

Get out of here!

He turned around to see if anyone was behind him, but he already knew there wouldn't be. The voice was inside and outside him all at once. It was like when he put a seashell against his ear. He could hear the sea and the sea was in the shell and in him. He felt cold and he shivered. He took a deep breath. He thought about hiding, but where could he go? He closed his eyes. If the voice had more to say, then let it say it. His father taught him to stand his ground when it came to fear. Alberto sat down on the edge of the bed. He placed his hands palms down on his thighs like someone who had been told to pay attention. Maybe a listening posture would make it easier for the voice to return, say what it had to say, then go away for good.

"Aquí estoy," he said. He crossed his arms to keep them from shaking.

After a while, he heard the microwave in the kitchen. Lupe was heating baby Chato's formula. There was a spiderweb in the corner of his room. He began to count the separate strands of filament: forty-five. Still no voice.

He decided to speak to it. Maybe the voice was like a bully. If you faced him, challenged him, he would let you be.

"Why get out of here?" he asked, in English.

He waited, both hoping and not hoping that there would be an answer. He knew how to wait. When he put a bowl inside the giant kiln that Don Andrés kept behind the pottery shop, waiting was all he could do. For every piece of ceramic, the wait was different. The good potter knew how to wait.

He heard a dog bark outside and then he heard Wayne curse. There was the sound of a toilet flushing and then of Lupe and Wayne speaking to each other. He gave the voice a few more moments to return and say whatever it needed to say and when nothing happened, he put his sneakers on and stepped out of his room.

Wayne was sitting at the kitchen table listening to voice mails on his cell phone. He had on athletic shorts and a New York Giants T-shirt. Lupe was pouring coffee into Wayne's mug with one hand and holding baby Chato on her hip.

"This damn woman is harassing me!" Wayne shouted

to no one or to everyone. Then, to Alberto: "I want you to go and clean her windows. She claims there are specks of paint all over the glass. I'm texting you her address. I told her you'd be there sometime this morning."

Alberto took baby Chato from Lupe's arms. Lupe gave Wayne the mug of coffee and then sat beside him. She waited for him to grab the mug, then said, "Wayne, it's Sunday." Wayne's full name was John Francis Wayne, but everyone called him Wayne.

"It's an hour's work tops and then he can go do whatever he wants! I gotta get this woman off my back!"

Tell him to go to hell!

Alberto was in the act of grabbing baby Chato's bottle when he heard the voice again. He hugged baby Chato closer to him. Lupe started to argue with Wayne. Baby Chato began to cry and for a moment Alberto thought that the baby had also heard the voice. He sat on the rocking chair in the living room and gave baby Chato his formula. For the first time since he'd heard the voice, it was clear to Alberto that it was not going to go away.

"Are you all right, hermanito?" Lupe came and sat across from him. Baby Chato was asleep again, his lips still clinging to the nipple of the bottle. "You look different."

"Different?" He felt different. The world didn't seem as solid as before. "How different?"

"You're pale, for one thing. It's like something's dragging you down."

Wayne had gone back to the bedroom. He could hear him shouting on the phone. Alberto noticed a trace of white powder on the coffee table.

"You can't do that anymore," Alberto said sternly.

"It was only a little coca. A tiny, tiny bit." Lupe made a sign with her thumb and index finger. "It keeps me from wanting more. Don't worry, hermanito."

Alberto reached out and checked Lupe's left arm. There were no new needle marks, but there was a yellow-and-purple bruise. "He hurt you again."

Lupe covered her arm with the sleeve of her bathrobe. Instead of responding to his comment, Lupe said, "I'm serious about you not being yourself. I don't know how long it's been since you went to the pottery studio or walked to Coney Island. When did you last go bowling with Jimbo? You don't sleep. I can hear you in your room crying or laughing, I can't tell which."

"I'm all right. Tired." Alberto rocked back and forth, looked down at baby Chato.

Lupe continued, lowering her voice. "I was doing

laundry yesterday and when I didn't see any of your laundry in the hamper, I went into your room and there was all your dirty laundry in the bottom of your closet. Your bed was unmade. There was an old, smelly banana peel on your desk!"

Alberto gave Lupe a questioning look.

"You have to admit, that's not you. You been cleaning up after yourself since you started to walk."

Alberto could not remember seeing a banana peel or even taking a banana to his room. And since when had he stopped making his bed as soon as he got up? The week before he had painted a whole wall, the last one to be painted in a room, the wrong shade of blue. Where was his mind during the two hours that it took him to paint the wall? It was as if there were clouds of forgetfulness in his mind. "I'm sorry."

"I'm not telling you this to give you a hard time. I'm telling you this because I want you to start caring about yourself more. I want you to put your room in order and then go to the pottery studio. I called them yesterday and paid for another month."

"That's so expensive. We need the money to send home."

"A few hours a week of studio time doesn't take away from what we send home."

"But . . ."

"After you finish the work Wayne asked you to do, go and make something beautiful like you used to do back home. Don't come back here."

Yeah! Don't come back!

"Stop!"

Alberto looked up and saw the surprised look on Lupe's face. How could he tell her that he wasn't talking to her without worrying her even more? He was embarrassed. And now Lupe had a worried look on her face. She was extending her arms, asking for baby Chato. Maybe she was afraid that he would hurt the baby. He removed the bottle from Chatito's mouth and handed the baby to Lupe. Alberto rubbed his right temple.

"And that's another thing. You've started talking to yourself."

"I'm practicing my English," Alberto responded.

"You do too much. All you do is work and study . . . and take care of Chatito. Go have some fun today. Go to a coffee shop and read your book. Go play soccer at the school. Then go see that lady with the windows. We'll be okay. Wayne promised to take us to Long Island. He has a house he wants to show me. Maybe . . ."

Lupe's hope for Wayne to do what was right, to be a good man, filled Alberto with sadness. From what he had seen, Wayne did not have it in him to be good. Alberto stood up quickly because he was afraid the sadness would bring back the voice. Lupe stood as well. They both turned toward the bedroom where Wayne was yelling on the phone.

"He's not good for you," Alberto said.

"I know, I know. I'm working on something. I got a plan. You know me. I always have a plan. But right now, he's all I got. All we got. Go now. I don't want you to be here when he comes out. He'll give you more work."

"No more coca, all right?" Alberto glared at Lupe. "Think of Chato."

"Okay, okay. Go. Please."

Alberto walked quickly to his room and grabbed the red duffel bag where he kept the materials he used for work: spatulas, rags, a can of thinner, window putty, a couple of paintbrushes, tape, a small roller, screwdriver, pliers. He took the white painter's overalls from the bottom of the closet and stuffed them in the bag. He looked around the room. On top of the dresser was a picture of his family taken at a Mérida carnival a week before his father died. His father had his arms around his mother and his sister Mercedes. Alberto's youngest sister, Chela, was standing next to a five-foot stuffed animal in the shape of a jaguar that Alberto had won for her. Lupe was not in the picture. Lupe was nineteen at the time and already struggling with addiction. She had managed to stop when she got pregnant, but the white powder on the table was a sign that she was opening the door to her hunger once again.

She's a maggot.

Alberto tried to block out the voice by concentrating on the image of his father in the picture. His father was trying to smile, but Alberto could see the look of worry and pain in his eyes. Was he thinking about Lupe? Or maybe his father somehow knew that he'd be dead the following week.

The five books he needed to prepare for the high school equivalency test were scattered on the floor next to his desk. One book for each of the subjects he needed to learn: reading, writing, social studies, science, and mathematics. On his nightstand there was the book on Japanese pottery. This little room and Lupe and Chato were all he had in this country. And they needed him. How could he not come back?

"It's what I got," he said out loud, hoping that the voice would hear him.

CHAPTER 2

Grace's mother, Miriam, had been calling and texting Wayne to send someone to clean the windows almost daily since they'd moved into the apartment the month before. Whoever painted the walls of the apartment got paint on the windowpanes. The smudges were particularly noticeable on the windows overlooking Prospect Park.

"Oh, hi, honey, I didn't know you were up!" Miriam said when she saw Grace in the living room.

"Was that Dad you were yelling at?" Grace was sitting on the new leather sofa, her legs tucked into an afghan of gold and maroon squares. She had a textbook open on her lap.

"That was the owner. I finally got ahold of the sleazy jerk and let him have it. I told him that for four thousand a month, I deserve a view unmarred by paint! He's sending someone over to clean them this morning."

Grace wondered for a moment whether *unmarred* was a word. Then she said, "They're coming today? It's Sunday."

"I know. That SOB's deliberately sending someone on Sunday morning just to spite me. But I had to say yes. Otherwise, who knows when we'd get the windows cleaned? To make matters worse, I have a meeting at the office at eleven." Miriam came over and sat on the edge of the sofa. She reached out and touched Grace's forehead. "Are you sick? You feel warm."

"It felt cold this morning." Grace pulled the afghan closer to her chest.

"You didn't tell me that you were skipping school on Thursday and Friday. Were you under the weather?" Grace moved her legs and a physics textbook fell on the floor. Miriam picked it up and handed it to her.

"I have a test tomorrow that counts for forty percent

of the semester's grade, and I've fallen behind. I stayed home on Thursday and Friday to catch up."

"Okay. But since when don't you tell me things?"

"I didn't think it was a big deal. How did you find out? Michael?"

"Michael called me to see if you were okay because he was worried about you. You didn't tell him you were skipping school either. He says he's been texting and leaving you voice mails."

"I'm okay."

"People worry. I worry. Your dad worries. He hasn't heard from you since . . ."

"He doesn't have the right to worry about me anymore."

"Oh, sweetie. I understand your anger. Trust me, I do. But it's not good. Not good for you mentally, physically, emotionally. Your anger is hurting *you* most of all." Miriam moved closer so she could hold Grace's hand. "Look at me. He doesn't want to be my husband, fine. But that doesn't mean he doesn't want to be your father."

Grace moved her hand out of Miriam's grasp. "Why did you let him take our home?"

"I didn't exactly let him. It wasn't just our home, it

was his office, his whole psychiatric practice, according to him. It was the only thing he wanted and I was tired of fighting." Miriam gestured toward the window. "This isn't so bad, is it? We'll make it ours. Once we get the windows clean." Miriam waited for Grace to smile. When the smile didn't come, she said: "It's not just anger that you feel, is it?"

Grace turned toward Miriam but looked past her to the gray sky beyond the window. "I don't understand how someone can say 'I don't love you anymore' and then leave."

"That's not exactly what he said. And anyway, he didn't say it to you, he said it to me."

Grace looked briefly at Miriam's anguished face and then out the window again. She continued, "This past week, it's as if what was clear before got hazy. Like I stepped into a fog. It's all blurry."

Miriam looked at Grace for a long time. Grace finally raised her eyes, and the look she saw was Miriam's kind but penetrating gaze. After a while, Miriam spoke.

"Do you think this sudden lack of clarity is affecting your relationship with Michael?"

"I'm not sure. Maybe."

There was a long silence. Then Miriam said softly, "If you're confused about love, join the club."

Grace smiled, a small smile.

"That's my girl. I haven't seen that smile in ages. Listen, a couple of things. You take your time figuring things out. Take a few more days off from school if you need to. What has helped me the most is to plow into work with blinders for anything else except the task at hand . . . and you. But you're not me . . . fortunately. Listen . . . I, uh, did something this morning, before this little talk; I asked Michael if he could come over and keep you company for a while."

"Mom!"

"I was worried about leaving you alone with the window cleaners. I wish I could stay home, but this is an emergency. We're terminating Lenny and this is the only time the rest of the partners can meet without him. We need to figure out what he's owed and what, if anything, we give him on top of that."

"You're letting sweet Lenny go? Why?"

"He's not producing," Miriam said sadly. "Sweet can be a problem in a private equity firm owned by five partners."

"And now only four. That will mean even more work for you."

"Not necessarily. Lenny's been creating extra . . ." Miriam stopped talking when they heard a knock on the door. Grace and Miriam exchanged a surprised look. No one ever knocked on their door. Visitors were announced by the security guard before they were allowed to take the elevator to the tenth floor.

Miriam jumped out of the sofa, walked to the door, and shouted: "Who is it?"

"For the windows." Grace heard the unmistakable foreign accent: *de weendows.*

Miriam glanced at the digital clock on the refrigerator. "It's only nine!" Then to Grace: "Crap! Are you decent?"

Grace removed the afghan to reveal her faded blue jeans and white T-shirt.

Miriam unlocked the door and opened it. "I didn't expect you so . . ."

It was difficult for Grace to imagine anything that would prevent Miriam from finishing a sentence, but when the boy stepped into the apartment, Grace understood that Miriam had been momentarily stunned just like she was.

He was Grace's age, maybe a year older. He was taller

than Miriam by a head and she had been the captain of her high school's volleyball team some twenty years ago. The boy, the young man, had the broad shoulders of an athlete, a swimmer perhaps. But what momentarily stopped Grace's breath was the dark, intense eyes. Grace had read about sparkling eyes in novels and considered the description an exaggeration, but this boy's eyes really did have a light in them. As if that wasn't enough, there was a gentleness about him that was warm and attractive.

"My name is Alberto, miss. Wayne told me to come about the windows."

The mention of Wayne snapped Miriam back from the rosy place she had momentarily visited. "Great. How long do you think it will take you?"

Alberto ignored Miriam's tone and turned his head toward the windows at the end of the room. "May I see?"

Miriam nodded. Alberto gave Grace a courteous smile as he walked past her, a simple smile acknowledging the presence of another human being. When he reached the windows, he began to touch the specks of paint with the tip of his index finger. He scratched one spot with his fingernail. Miriam, standing next to him, said, "They're disgusting! The super downstairs refused to do anything. He said the glass had tint that would be scratched if not done correctly. He told me to call the landlord so he could send a professional. So . . . are you the professional and can you get it all done this morning?"

"Are all the windows like this?" Alberto spoke without looking at Miriam.

"Every last one of them. I told your boss about them when we inspected the property prior to moving in. It should have been done the next day."

"I'm sorry." Alberto looked at Miriam briefly and then turned away.

"You're sorry?"

"The people who painted did not do it with care." He talked slowly, enunciating every word, as if he thought Miriam might be heard of hearing. "It will need to be done carefully."

"More than a couple of hours?"

"Maybe. If you want it done correct."

Miriam was silent for a moment and then she relaxed. It seemed to Grace as if her mother had surrendered to the boy's good sense. "What's your last name?" Miriam asked, her tone softer. Miriam always asked for the last names of the people who did work for her. It made them more accountable.

"Bocel, miss." He gave Miriam a small nod. Alberto lowered the duffel bag to the floor. Miriam walked back to the sofa and sat next to Grace. They watched Alberto take out a plastic water bottle, a white rag, and a small spatula. He wet the rag with something that smelled like alcohol. He rubbed the rag on the paint and delicately removed the paint with the spatula. One spot, the size of a dime, took him a couple of minutes to remove.

Miriam sighed and then said, "Will you be all right? Michael's not coming until eleven. I really do have to go to this meeting, and I don't want to leave you alone."

"Really, Mom? Does he look dangerous to you?" Alberto was on his knees now, dampening a smudge on the bottom pane.

"I was worried about *him*." How long since Grace had heard her mother laugh? Last year, maybe?

"I'll be all right, Mom. Go to your meeting. Put poor Lenny out on the street." Grace pointed at Alberto with her chin. "I doubt he'll even notice I'm here."

"He's focused, isn't he?"

Grace picked up the physics book, placed it on her lap, and pretended to read. "Like me."

Twenty minutes later, Grace went over to the hall closet, took out a two-step ladder, and placed it next to

Alberto. He jumped back and gasped when he sensed someone next to him. "I'm sorry, I didn't mean to scare you," Grace said, taking a step back from him. Alberto placed his hand on his heart to quiet it down. It was an endearing gesture that Grace had never seen performed by a man. Then relief came over Alberto's face, as if he were glad that it was only the girl from the sofa.

"This will make it easier for you to reach the top frames," Grace said.

"Thank you. That's very nice of you."

Grace stood there nodding as if agreeing that, of course, it was nice of her. She blinked and then forced herself to speak. "I'm Grace. Sometimes people call me Gracie."

"Greesy."

"*Gray* like the color and *sí* like yes. Gray-sí."

Alberto smiled. But Grace wasn't sure whether he had understood. Then he said, "Grace like gracias." He glanced at the ladder. "Gracias, Grace."

"You're welcome. Alberto, right? I'll be there, studying. I hope that's okay. Let me know if you need anything."

When Grace turned to go back to the sofa, Miriam

was by the hallway doing the *tsk, tsk* sign with her fingers. "Studying hard?"

"I was just trying to be helpful," Grace said, and stuck out her tongue.

"I have to go, honey. There's leftover pasta from last night that you can microwave for lunch. Or make yourself a sandwich. I'll be back early." Miriam bent over and kissed the top of Grace's head. "Study hard. Princeton is waiting."

"I will."

"Oh, by the way, about this morning and about love."

"That's okay, Mom. I didn't mean to burden you."

"Oh, please." Miriam lowered her voice. "I welcome being burdened by you. I sure as hell am not an expert on love matters, but . . . talk to Michael. About your confusion. Confusion about feelings gets worse, sometimes beyond repair, if you don't talk about it. That's my two cents." Miriam took Grace into her arms and whispered: "I love you. There's zero confusion about that."

"I love you too," Grace said.

After Miriam left, Grace tried to study but ended up watching Alberto in silence. At one point, she noticed that he shook his head and said no. It was a clear no and it was loud enough for her to hear. She expected him to turn around and look for her reaction, but he simply kept on working. After a while, Grace saw him take a step back and inspect the window. Then he turned, took a few steps toward the sofa, and said, "May I have a glass of water, please?"

"Yes, of course." Grace rose quickly and went to the kitchen. She got a glass, filled it with ice and then water from the dispenser on the refrigerator. When he took the glass, Grace noticed a tremor in his hand, and there were drops of perspiration on his forehead. He drank the water all at once and then rattled the ice cubes a little, as if delighting in the sound they made. He handed Grace the empty glass with the same look of delight.

"Más?" Grace asked.

"No, gracias," he responded, his face beaming. "Usted habla español?"

"Poquito." Grace was on the verge of telling him that she had taken four years of high school Spanish when she saw him raise his right hand to his ear and shut his eyes. "Are you okay?"

Alberto didn't seem to hear her question. He smiled at Grace and then quickly looked around the room until his eyes fell on a small porcelain bowl on the glass table next to the sofa. He walked over and knelt to inspect it closely. "Ahh, so beautiful."

"From Japan. My mother said it's hand-painted." Grace remembered the explanation her mother gave when Grace had asked why it had cost six thousand dollars.

"Yes." There were dozens of small purple, blue, pink flowers on a bowl the size of a grapefruit. But what amazed Alberto the most was the small indentation in the porcelain created for each flower.

Grace picked up the bowl and offered it to Alberto. "You can hold it."

He placed the bowl in the palm of his left hand as if it were a small bird that just happened to land there. Grace noticed how the hand trembled. Alberto carefully returned the bowl to the table. Then, unexpectedly, he said, "One day I try to make a thing like this so beautiful."

"You do ceramics?"

"In Ticul, Mexico. That was my work."

"Oh. Do you do it here?"

"Sometimes. Today, maybe. After here. The studio is nearby." His eyes fell on the bowl again. "I have a book on Japanese pottery. The bowl is from Arita."

"Arita?"

"A place in Japan with special clay. It is very precious."
He stopped, embarrassed, like one who had just caught
himself showing off. "Excuse me. I prevent you from
studying."

"No, no," Grace said quickly. "I would like to know more."

"That's all I know," Alberto said apologetically. "I only
read five pages."

Alberto laughed first, and then Grace.

There was a moment when Grace and Alberto looked
at each other and then quickly away. Grace could not
think of one single thing to say. That was unusual for her.

"I can do the back windows now," Alberto said. "It's
okay if I go?"

"Oh, sure. I'll show you." Alberto picked up the duffel bag and followed Grace down the hallway. "We have
three bedrooms. My mother's, mine, and a guest room
my mother uses as an office. The two bathrooms here in
the hall and in my mother's room don't have windows,
so you're in luck."

Grace waited for him to say something, but Alberto
only smiled, and Grace wasn't sure whether he had
caught her small attempt at humor. They stopped at the
doorway of one of the bedrooms. "You will never know
it by the looks of this room, but I'm not a messy person.

In fact, the opposite. I'm—" Grace rushed into the room and removed a bra from the back of her desk chair. But Alberto did not seem to have noticed. His eyes were fixed on the windowpanes that lined one side of the bedroom. There was buzzing coming from the intercom by the front door of the apartment. "That must be my . . . friend. Well, if you need anything . . ."

Just before she turned to leave, Alberto said, "Gracias."

"De nada," Grace responded. On the way to the front door, she said to herself: *He's going to think I'm a slob.*

CHAPTER 3

Michael put his hands on his hips and struck a model's pose when Grace opened the door. He was dressed in white shorts, a light blue polo shirt, and a yellow sweater tied around his shoulders. "What do you think?"

"Snazzy," Grace said. "You look like someone out of *The Great Gatsby*."

Michael grabbed Grace gently by the shoulders. "Are you okay?"

"Yes." When Michael continued to peer into her eyes, Grace added, "I think I'm coming down with something."

"Three days without even a single text. A tiny emoji?"

"I know. I'm sorry. I have no good or bad excuse."

"I understand." Michael leaned in and kissed Grace. "But please don't ever do that again." Michael waited for Grace to nod and then headed to the refrigerator, where he took out a Diet Coke. "You know what I've discovered?" He opened the can and took a sip. Grace went back to the sofa. "I play better when I dress like a pro. I'm more confident."

"I'm sorry my mother dragged you away from your game. There was no need, really."

Michael sat on the beige leather armchair in front of Grace. He leaned over and placed the Diet Coke on the end table near the Arita bowl that Alberto had just noticed. Michael dug out a cell phone from his shorts pocket. He tapped on the screen as he spoke. "Do you mind if I answer this text from my dad?"

Grace nodded. She opened her physics book but kept her eyes on Michael. She wondered what Michael meant when he said that he "understood" why she had not answered any of his messages or texts when she herself did not understand. She had followed an instinct that urged her to be alone, to feel what she was feeling without disguising it with politeness. But what was she feeling? Her mother thought it was anger at her father, at moving out of their town house, but it didn't feel like anger, not exactly. It was more like a bitter kind of sadness and a disturbing dislike for things and people she had liked before. Michael's thumbs were dancing over his phone. She remembered the first time he'd texted her. He asked if she would go with him and his family to watch the men's finals at the US Open. The week before she had noticed him looking at her during tennis practice. She knew who he was. Everyone at school knew Michael. He had been a sophomore like her and already the best player on the school's tennis team. He was also gorgeous, with his longish blond hair and baby-blue eyes. He could have asked dozens of other girls and they would have gladly said yes. But he asked her, and her heart was jolted by joy.

Michael put the phone on his lap and reached for the Diet Coke. He took a long sip, placed the can back on the table. "My dad wants me to have dinner with him tonight. He's been after me to work at his law firm this summer even though I've already accepted an offer from Cravath. I don't know what to do. I don't want to hurt his feelings, but how do you compare a five-lawyer firm with one of the largest and most prestigious firms in the country?"

"Maybe your dad really needs you right now? Didn't he just lose his best paralegal?"

"I know, I know. But it's Cravath! Am I supposed to turn them down for a paralegal job?"

"You have so many summers ahead of you before you start practicing law. You can try different jobs. That way, you can be sure of what you really like."

Michael gave Grace the kind of look you give someone who says something totally out of character. And, when she thought about it, it was possible that he was right. Michael continued tapping his phone. "I just texted him. I told him I would think about it." Michael exhaled, tried to calm himself. He looked around this room. "Of course, you know what he really wants."

"For you to be happy?"

"Yeah, but it's his own version of happiness. He wants me to join his firm and take over when he retires."

"But he's never asked you that."

"Mom told me. Apparently, he's been secretly hoping for that since, I don't know. When did I decide to be a lawyer?"

"Kindergarten?"

"Funny. He knows I've always wanted to work on

corporate takeovers. I can only do that in the biggest firms. Am I supposed to give up my dream for his?"

Grace sighed. It was the wrong time to answer any questions about dreams.

"So," Michael said after a while, "where's the window washer I'm supposed to protect you from?"

"He's doing the windows in my room," Grace said. "He's nice." Then, trying unsuccessfully to not sound annoyed: "I don't think I need protection." Grace opened the textbook and tried to focus. *Boltzmann constant. Entropy. Equipartition.* The words danced in front of her, unable to find any footing in her brain. What was going on? Why did Michael's unwillingness to help his father suddenly bug her so much? Was she seeing things correctly or was Michael, deep down, as self-centered as her father?

"Listen to this," Michael said, animated. "My father just texted me back. 'A journey of a thousand miles begins with a single step.' What does that mean? Jonathan was telling me over tennis that his father is going to give him a Land Rover for graduation. Jonathan's going to Rutgers! Rutgers! I'm going to Harvard. What do I get? Quotes by Confucius!"

"I could very easily flunk physics." Grace was looking out the spotless bay window when she said this.

"You have to look at this rationally." She heard Michael's voice as if he were speaking from the other side of the window. She turned slowly toward him. He was looking at her with concern in his eyes. His voice had the same kindness he used when he showed her ways to improve her tennis game. "There's one more month left of school. You've worked so hard all these years. Just give it a little more gas. Get an A in physics and you're a shoo-in for valedictorian. Buckle down a little longer."

Grace closed the book and placed it on the table next to the Arita bowl. She waited for Michael to look up from his phone. "Do you know what I've been thinking about these past couple of days?"

"Yes," Michael said softly.

"What?"

"You're thinking of quitting school."

"Close," Grace said, surprised.

"You have senioritis. You're sick of studying. You're going to Princeton in September; there's nothing to strive for anymore. You've lost your motivation. You know, I hate to bring this up, but I seem to remember advising you way back when not to leave AP Physics for the last semester."

Grace exhaled. Was that what was happening to her? Michael was right about one thing: She had lost her motivation. Working to get one more A so she could be valedictorian seemed silly. It wasn't silly three months ago, but now it was. "Senioritis," she said quietly.

Michael placed the phone on the coffee table and moved to the edge of his chair. "Your dad up and left you and your mom. That's enough to derail anybody."

Grace was grateful for Michael's caring tone. "Dad served my mother with divorce papers a year ago. I never lost motivation, as you put it. Why now?"

"Because now the divorce has become real for you. It's one thing to know your parents are getting divorced and another to lose your home."

"So he's just another jerk out for himself?"

Michael smiled, a sad smile. He moved over to the sofa next to Grace and took her hand. "Grace, you've got to get past him. Remember last semester—the tournament at the Westchester Country Club? You were losing the final match. One more game, one more point, and you were out. I remember the look on your face during the break. You were determined to win and you did.

That's what you need now; you've got to summon that determination one more time. Maybe your father *is* a jerk. Maybe he's just a flawed human being like the rest of us. Whoever he is, don't let him drag you down."

"Julie Kim," Grace said.

"What?"

"That was the name of the girl I beat. She was nice."

"I'm just saying that one of the things I most admire about you is your commitment to accomplishing what you set out to do. That's what you need to rely on right now."

Grace squeezed Michael's hand and then removed hers from his grasp. She lifted the afghan from where it lay at her feet and covered her legs. "Michael. I've been thinking . . ."

There was a rattling noise coming from the back of the apartment. Michael stood. "I'll go check."

"It's okay," Grace said, "it's just the blinds. They crash down on me all the time."

"Doesn't hurt to check," Michael said as he walked down the hall. A few seconds later Grace heard Michael giving instructions to Alberto. Michael was speaking loudly and slowly, as if Alberto were a child. "You pull this string here. See? Like this. Pull. String."

"Everything okay?" Grace asked when he returned. "You were gone a long time."

"I stayed to watch him clean one of the windowpanes. He looked like he was performing brain surgery on the glass." Michael squinted and imitated Alberto meticulously scraping a speck of paint.

"He's very focused," Grace said.

"Something's not totally right with him." Michael sat on the leather chair and crossed his legs. "When I first went in there, he was whispering something in Spanish I couldn't understand. He turned around with a scared look on his face when he heard me. By the way, I saw that your mother's Patek Philippe watch was right there next to her bed."

"You're telling me this because . . ."

"I could go in there and get it for you. You don't want it to get stolen."

"Michael," Grace said, ignoring his words, "there's something I want to talk to you about, something that I've been thinking these past couple of days. I'd like your honest opinion."

Michael's phone vibrated in his hand. He looked at it. "I'm sorry. Do you mind? It's my mom."

Michael walked to the window and talked into his

phone in a low whisper. Grace saw him place the palm of his hand on the spotless glass. "Mom, please!" she heard him say. Michael stuck the phone in his pocket. "They've joined forces," Michael said, walking past Grace on the way to the kitchen. "She wants me to work with Dad this summer. Says I owe it to him." He opened the door to the refrigerator, took out another Diet Coke, and opened it. The can hissed and sprayed gas and soda on Michael's face. "Damn it!" Michael yelled as he dropped the can on the floor. Grace stood slowly and went over to him. "What is it?" Michael asked angrily.

It took Grace a moment to realize that Michael was not speaking to her. She turned and saw Alberto standing in the hallway. "Excuse me, miss." Alberto's eyes remained fixed on Grace. "Is everything all right?"

"Yeah. Everything is just dandy!" Michael shouted.

"Michael!" Grace glared at Michael. Then to Alberto: "It was just an accident. Thank you for checking."

"If you need me, let me know," Alberto said softly. Alberto kept his eyes fixed on Michael for a few seconds before turning around and walking back to Miriam's bedroom.

Grace waited until Alberto was gone and then handed Michael a roll of paper towels. She went back to the sofa and sat again. She was quiet. She waited for Michael to finish cleaning and then waited for him to speak when he finally sat down.

"I'm sorry. The combination of my mother's call and the can exploding . . ."

"You were kind of rude to Alberto."

"Alberto? Oh, I didn't mean to sound rude. I lost it there for a second. I'm sorry. This thing with my parents has me on edge. I don't know what to do." He stopped himself. "There was something you were about to tell me before Mom called."

"Maybe this isn't the right time."

"I'd like to hear whatever it is." Michael waited, and when Grace still did not speak, he said, "I know something is going on with you. Why would you go three whole days without a single text? In the two and a half years that we've been together, you have never, ever done that."

"I know."

"Grace, you're not having doubts about us, are you? Oh my God. Grace, we've made plans. We've talked so much about staying together long-distance when we're in college. I thought—"

"I know."

"You know? But what, then?"

Grace took a deep breath. "Princeton. Medical school. They're not as solid as they used to be. Maybe I should defer college for a year."

"You serious?" Michael asked, alarmed.

"I could maybe volunteer at a hospital to see if I liked . . ."

"What about us? Are we solid?"

"Us?"

"As in you and me?"

Grace felt the tears come. "Everything seems . . . I don't know. It's as if I'm in a theater and the curtain opens and I see me acting out my future following lines and directions that were written by someone else. I don't feel like I've chosen what I am setting out to do. I don't even know if I've chosen who I want to be. Do you know what I mean?"

"Okay, but there's a reason we've been together these two and a half years, right? What's the reason?"

"What's the reason?"

"I love you and you love me. That's the reason."

"Yes, love." It occurred to Grace just then that all she really knew about love was that it was possible for it to end.

"I'm not sure what you're trying to say here. What are you trying to say? What do you want to do?"

Grace used a corner of the afghan to wipe her cheeks. "I don't think we should have this conversation right now. I'm not thinking clearly and . . ."

Michael stood. He looked to Grace as if he suddenly did not know where he was. He slowly sat down. "These doubts about us . . . I never expected them. Let's . . . let's just pause this. Take a few days off. This isn't *you* doubting. It's not you. You're confusing me with your father or something. Grace, we *chose* each other because we're perfect for each other. We're partners. I support you in your goals and you support me. We dreamt a future together and are working for it. I see you in the future. That's how I know I love you. Maybe you're right. This may not be the right time for this conversation. I'm rattled from the summer job thing. Let's all calm down. Give each other some space. Okay, I'm going to go now."

"Michael . . ." Grace stretched out her hand but didn't stand up.

Michael didn't take it. "No, let's not say anything more. This is just one of those things that happens to couples. We'll be okay. We'll be okay. I know it. We're part of each other now. I'll go now. Don't say anything, please."

Grace watched Michael walk out the door. She had hurt him. She could have done more to assure him that their "us" was still solid. But how could she when her whole world was cracking? Something inside her kept urging her to be true to her brokenness.

Truth was the only mend.

CHAPTER 4

The voice spoke to Alberto twice while he was in Grace's apartment. Once, when he was cleaning the window facing the park, the voice told him to jump. Alberto instinctively responded no. No, he would not do what the voice asked, and no, the voice should not speak to him, especially when people were around. The second time the voice spoke, Alberto was in the mother's bedroom, and he heard someone shout. He became concerned that the boy who came to the apartment was hurting Grace. The voice said, *She's nothing.*

When he finished cleaning the last window, Alberto

took off his white overalls and placed the rags and tools into the red bag. He was walking down the hall when he heard Grace and Michael talking. It sounded like a serious conversation, and he did not want to interrupt. He went back to the mother's bedroom and waited until he heard a door close. When he came out again, Grace was quietly crying. He stood at the entrance to the living room not knowing what to do or say.

"Grace," he said, after a while.

"Oh, hi," she said, quickly wiping her eyes and standing up. "I'm sorry. I didn't know you were there."

"I intruded on you."

"One of those boyfriend and girlfriend things, you know? It happens." Grace stuck her hands in the pockets of her jeans and then took them out. "You all done? Do I need to pay you? I don't know how this works."

"No, no. No payment." Alberto gestured no with his hand. "It's all taken care of." He began to walk toward the door, but Grace's unsuccessful attempt at smiling stopped him. "Will you be okay?"

"Oh, yes. Absolutely. Thank you. Thank you for asking."

Alberto nodded. He took another step toward the door and then turned to face Grace. "You don't look like you should be alone now. Why don't you come do some pottery? The studio is across the park. I can show you or you can just watch. It will rest your mind."

Grace let out a small laugh. "Is it so obvious?"

"Pardon me?"

"Is it so obvious that my mind's a wreck? Thank you, but I can't. I need to crack down on the books. I have a big exam next week."

"You'll study better after pottery. You'll see."

"It sounds as if you're speaking from experience."

Alberto touched his forehead. "My mind needs rest too."

Grace was silent for a moment, reflecting. "Okay," she finally said. "I'll bring my book and go to the library afterward."

They stood side by side in front of Grace's building looking at the park. It was as if each were thinking the same thing. It was beautiful to see the baby leaves on the trees. Behind the trees they could see ducks floating on a lake. They walked to the nearest stoplight and crossed Ocean Avenue. They both headed toward a bench overlooking the lake.

"Are you hungry?" Alberto asked on the way there. "My sister made me a sandwich."

"Is it lunchtime already? I've lost all track of time. I'm not hungry, but you go ahead."

Alberto looked up and searched for the sun, but the clouds were hiding it. "I'm not hungry either."

"Can we sit here for a few moments?" Grace asked. "This is so peaceful. I can't believe I've never been here before."

Just before sitting down, Alberto turned and pointed at Grace's apartment. "You can see this spot from your home."

"My home," Grace repeated absentmindedly. "Lately it feels like a prison."

"I'm sorry," Alberto said softly.

"No, no. I'm the one that's sorry. I don't know what's come over me lately. Let's sit down. Tell me something else. Something about you."

"I wish I knew the names of all the trees in Brooklyn," Alberto said when they were both seated. "I recognize the oaks by the pointed leaves and the birches by their white bark. But that's about all."

"I'm not much better and I've lived here all my life."

"That small tree with pink buds reminds me of the flamboyán outside my house. I always liked how the morning sun lit the flamboyán's branches as if they were on fire."

"You must miss home very much."

"Yes. Sometimes more than others."

Go back to Mexico!

Alberto winced.

"You okay?" Grace asked.

"My head sometimes hurts from the solvent I use on the windows." What would it be like to tell Grace about the voice? Would she run away from him? "The fresh air is good."

Grace took a deep breath. "It smells like salt air."

"That's because it's going to rain." Alberto licked his index finger and raised it above his head. "In maybe two hours, the rain will come."

Grace made a disbelieving face.

"It's true," Alberto said, laughing. "Ticul's a couple of hours from the sea, but when the air smells like the ocean, rain comes."

"We'll see," she said, smiling. Then: "I'm sorry about this morning. Michael is usually polite and considerate. He was preoccupied with family stuff."

He's a dumbass like you!

"Captain America." The words popped out of Alberto's mouth.

"What?"

"I don't know why I just thought of this comic book that someone gave me once. The man who gave it to me, his name was Mr. Ramsey. He was one of Wayne's tenants. Mr. Ramsey was on his way to a nursing home when Wayne sent me to help him clean out the apartment. He was very, how do you say, grumpy. I didn't like him, and I didn't think he liked me. Then when I was leaving, he gave me a Captain America comic book. The comic book was inside a plastic bag. He said it was valuable and wanted me to have it."

"People are not always what they seem," Grace said.

"Sometimes they are better and sometimes they are worse. That man, Mr. Ramsey, was like my grandfather back home. Hard on the outside, but soft inside."

Alberto noticed the sad expression on Grace's face. "This conversation is not resting your mind. We should go do pottery."

"I was just thinking about my grandfather. He lives nearby and I haven't seen him in four years. Tell me something else. About Ticul or about pottery. Do you have family here? Where do you live?"

"You're a good person, Grace."

"How do you know?"

"You talk to me."

"That's it? That's all I have to do to be a good person?"

"You talk to me like I'm someone like you. Not just the painter." Alberto paused. "And you put ice in my water."

Grace giggled and shook her head.

"I paint so many apartments. I don't know how many. People give us water. But never ice. Even people with refrigerators that make ice, they give us water from the faucet. I think that makes you kind. I hope is okay for me to speak like this."

"Like what?"

"Like I'm your friend."

Grace started to say something and then caught herself. "Let's go do some pottery."

They stood at the same time. Alberto sounded confused when he spoke. "There must be a way to go through the park, but I don't know the paths. I usually go around."

"Okay," Grace said. When they got to the sidewalk, a convertible full of girls honked and hooted at Alberto. Grace glanced over at him and he shrugged, embarrassed.

They walked in silence.

Alberto stopped to admire a group of trees with brilliant white flowering branches. "What kind of tree is that?"

"Those are cherry blossoms," Grace said.

"You *do* know the names of some trees," Alberto joked.

"Cherry blossoms. Everybody knows those!"

"What I would like to learn someday is how to paint trees like that on ceramic."

"What's stopping you?"

"Work. Work that pays enough for me to send money to my mother and two sisters in Mexico. You asked where I live. I live with my sister Lupe and her baby in Flatbush. The father of the baby is Wayne, the owner of your building."

"Oh."

"You know Wayne?"

"I met him once. He's sleazy."

"Sleesie?"

"Sleazy. Like you want to take a shower after you talk to him."

"Ah! Sleazy. That's a good word for Wayne."

Get away from this bitch!

"Alberto?"

"Huh?"

"You should get those headaches checked. Do you wear a mask when you work?"

"Lupe thinks Wayne is sleazy too. But she stays with him. For the sake of the baby. Maybe for my sake too. But no more talk about sad things. You want to know what I like the most about pottery?"

"Yes. It's also okay to talk about whatever you want."

"When I make pottery, I concentrate. I pay attention to how my hands touch the clay, how to move my fingers so I can make the clay match the picture that's in my mind. It's a happy concentration. It's not like those books I have for the high school equivalency exam where I need to figure out what time Lucy and Joey meet when they travel in trains going in opposite directions at different speeds. That kind of concentration is hard. But making pottery? It's like being with a good friend."

Grace said hesitantly, "Do you have friends . . . like that . . . here in Brooklyn, I mean?"

Alberto immediately thought of Chatito, but it felt strange to tell Grace that his best friend was a baby. Then, after a few more seconds, he said, "A boy in my painting crew. His name is Jimbo. Sometimes we go bowling together on Sundays. He tells me about his life in Haiti. I tell him about Ticul."

Grace said, "I've never gone bowling."

"No?"

Alberto and Grace looked at each other and blushed simultaneously. Neither one knew what to say.

Then they laughed.

CHAPTER 5

*Y*ou're back!" a woman behind the counter in the pottery studio shouted as soon as Alberto opened the door. "We missed you! People have been asking about you." Alberto held the door for Grace to enter. "And you brought a friend."

"This is Grace," Alberto said. "I'm sorry, I have forgotten your name."

"That breaks my heart." The woman placed a hand on her chest and made a sad face. "Carol," she said with a smile. Carol walked to a shelf and carefully picked up a black teapot. She placed it on the counter in front of

Alberto and waited for Alberto to react. Alberto stared at the teapot and then at Carol. "You made this. Last time you were here. Remember?"

On Alberto's face, Grace saw a look of blankness.

"This is a teapot I made in Ticul," Alberto muttered.

"No, no. I saw you make it. I was amazed and still am. I put it in the kiln just like you asked. I can't tell you how many people have asked me about this. They can't believe someone who comes to my studio made this. It's . . . it's magnificent. Just look at the lid; it fits perfectly, the handle, the spout. It's the work of an expert."

"I made this? Here?" Alberto asked, doubtful.

"He's being modest," Carol said to Grace. "I've never seen anything like it." Then to Alberto, "I'll keep it for you while you work. Is a pound of clay enough?"

Alberto nodded.

At a nearby table, Grace saw three women whispering in the direction of Alberto. Grace turned to watch Alberto. How could women, young and old, resist looking at him? He stood out. The color of his skin, his height, the gentleness of his movements were impossible to ignore.

Carol took out a small shovel and dug out a lump of clay from a white plastic bucket. She weighed the clay on a scale and handed it to Alberto. "Now go make something beautiful," she told him.

They found a table in front of the three women. Alberto stood while Grace sat on one of the stools. Alberto divided the clay into two pieces and gave one to Grace. "It's hard," Grace said as she tried to imitate Alberto's kneading motion.

"Go slow. Little by little the clay adjusts to your hands. It's easier when you stand up. That way you can use your whole body." Alberto rocked slightly on his feet as he pushed down on the clay.

"Hey, Alberto, what are you making today?" one of the women behind them asked.

Alberto turned and shrugged. "We'll see."

"You're very popular," Grace teased.

Alberto murmured, a worried tone in his voice. "I don't remember their names. Their faces look familiar. I've been here many times and I didn't remember Carol's name. And that teapot. I'm certain I made it in Ticul. But how did it get here? That's a complicated piece to make. It would have taken me a whole day to make."

"Maybe all those fumes from the solvents you use to clean windows are making you lose your mind," Grace joked. Alberto turned to her, a scared look on his face. "I forget people's names all the time," Grace added quickly. "We can only keep track of so many things. So, what *are* you making?"

"What would you like, Grace? Something for you to remember this day."

"Really? Something for me?" Grace felt warmth rise to her face. She wanted to say that it was unlikely she would forget this day, but instead said, "I don't know. I already have everything." *I already have everything. Did I seriously just say that?* "I mean . . ."

Alberto's laugh stopped her. "You don't have *everything*. You don't have a small bowl with a lid to put your earrings in. I saw the earrings on the window shelf in your bedroom."

"On the window shelf?" Grace exclaimed. "No wonder I'm always losing those things! Can you make that? Isn't that difficult?"

"Very," Alberto said, pretending to frown. "And what do you want to make, Grace?"

"Oh gosh. Would it be okay if I just watch you? I'll learn more that way."

"Let's make it together." Alberto walked to a nearby counter and picked a few tools from a plastic tub. He filled a small bowl with water, found a sponge and a rag, and then dug his fingers into the cool clay. "This clay has more plastic than the orange barro I worked with at home. Here. Feel how it sticks to your fingers." Alberto lifted his hands so that Grace could touch the ball he was making.

"It's warm," Grace observed.

"The heat comes from my hands. Feel." Alberto opened his hands so that Grace could place her palms on top of them.

"They're hot!" Grace made a sizzling sound. *What exactly is happening here?* She returned, with effort, to what Alberto was saying.

"The clay at home comes from mines on the outskirts of Ticul. Don Andrés, the owner of the shop where I worked, used to say that the clay had to be loved slowly and carefully by kneading and adding small amounts of water and kneading some more and then waiting. Love takes time."

Grace swallowed. She tried to speak, but the feeling that invaded her made it impossible.

"Are you all right? Your face is red, like you have a fever." Alberto tried to touch her forehead, but Grace involuntarily stepped away from him.

"This is unexpected," Grace said to herself. She placed her hand over her heart as if to keep it from jumping out.

"What is unexpected?"

Grace took a deep breath. "I . . . didn't expect to be . . . so interested . . . in . . . this process."

Alberto smiled. A knowing smile. Grace was sure he could see what she was feeling. "Do what I do," Alberto said, and began pressing on the ball of clay, rolling it, making spheres of different sizes. Grace tried to imitate the motion of Alberto's fingers, but her fingers were not strong enough. She pounded her ball of clay with her fist. Alberto placed his hand on hers. He opened her fingers one by one and then wrapped her hand around the clay. There was a moment when Grace thought about moving her hand, but there was something intense and soothing about his touch and all she could do was try to catch her breath.

Alberto flattened a small ball of clay with the palm of his hand and then he cut it into a rectangle the size of a postcard. Grace did the same. "This will be the base for the jewelry box." Then he took a small chunk from one of the balls and made a coil, his hands moving inward and outward. They both worked in silence. Alberto's movements were graceful, Grace's clumsy. Alberto's coil was perfectly formed. Grace thought her coil looked like an underfed worm. Out of that coil they made four pieces, which he joined to the base.

"It's like a building a log cabin," Grace said.

Now and then, Alberto would look up and smile at Grace. It was obvious to Grace that he had no need to speak, and she was surprised at how comfortable she was with him quietly working next to her. She took the coil she was making and began to shape it into a bowl.

It would be her own gift for Alberto. A thank-you for the new sense of aliveness she was feeling.

"When Don Andrés first let me work on pottery, he had me making calaveras, skulls, for the Día de los Muertos, which is what tourists most like to buy. I tried and tried but they would come out so ugly that I was afraid to show them to Don Andrés. I hid them so he couldn't find them."

Grace looked at the lopsided clump of something she was making. "I think I know the feeling."

Alberto went on. "But one day when I was coming to work, I saw my calaveras in the front of the store. Don Andrés found them and said they were perfect. 'With calaveras, the uglier the better.'"

"I'm not exactly sure how to take that," Grace said.

Their eyes met and they laughed.

"Actually, the calaveras were so bad nobody bought them. Now I think Don Andrés wanted me to have a good regard for my work. All of it. If I really tried, it was good."

"You seem happy here, working with clay. Happier than when you were cleaning our windows."

Alberto looked up and around as if looking for someone. "I am happy now." Then: "Someday, when I save enough money, I'll go back to Ticul and buy the shop from Don Andrés. He'll be ready to retire by then."

"Is that what you want?"

"It's a dream. It's a long way off. Painting doesn't pay very much, and I want to pass the high school equivalency exam. My mind . . . it works slow. And now, more and more, I forget things. It will take many years. And you, Grace? Do you have a dream?"

Grace sighed. "I thought I did. But lately . . . I have doubts."

"My father used to say la duda es la madre de la fe. Doubt is the mother of faith."

"Ha! I'll have to think about that one. Your father is in Ticul?"

"He died." Alberto picked up a lump of clay and squeezed it.

"I'm sorry."

"It was an accident." Alberto's eyes reddened and then he turned all his attention to the clay. Grace felt a warm, vibrant energy pulling her to Alberto. It was clear and powerful like a rushing brook. A fear rose in her. What was happening? She quickly finished shaping the bowl and then she took a wet sponge and smoothed the surface, just like Alberto was doing to the sides of the box. "This has been very lovely," she said, holding the oddly shaped bowl in her hand, "but I have this exam tomorrow and . . . I should call Michael. I wasn't very nice to him this morning."

Alberto took Grace's creation from her hand. "This is beautiful."

"It looks a little deformed," Grace said sadly.

"But *you* made it. I'll put it in the kiln with the jewelry box I'm making. They won't be done today. I need to make a lid for your jewelry box and then come back next week to glaze it. How can I get them to you? I can take them to your apartment."

"Leave them here. With Carol. I walk by all the time. I can pick them up. I'm so sorry, I really do have to go now. It's been so nice to know you . . . my mind is totally, a hundred percent more restful. Okay. Bye now."

Alberto held out a hand, but Grace did not reach for it. She wiggled her fingers, indicating goodbye, and hurried out. When she was outside, she turned and saw Alberto smiling at the bowl she had made. What was she doing? She should rush back in there and reenter the safe and loving space she had occupied for the past hour. It was a mistake to leave, and it was a mistake to stay. For a moment, she imagined what Michael would say of her bowl. Would he admire it simply because she'd made it? She looked at Alberto one last time and then walked in the direction of the library.

CHAPTER 6

Grace sat at a table in the middle of the library's large reading room. That spot was as distant as possible from the obviously homeless people who occupied the room. One of them, a woman two tables away, angrily pointed at an invisible adversary.

Grace remembered that not more than a week ago, she had wanted to be a psychiatrist like her father. When people asked her why, she answered, "To help people." But there in front of her were the kind of people she would need to help, and they scared her.

She flipped through the pages of her physics notebook and saw how each page contained elaborate doodles. The doodles were mostly squares and circles of different sizes. One page consisted of one square that was filled in with hundreds of tiny bubbles. Little meticulously constructed honeycombs, safe-looking prisons—perfect in their own way.

What happened to me at the pottery studio? It was so uncomplicated. A crush. An infatuation. It happens. Why should I be exempt?

Grace shook her head. Was there such a big difference between the woman arguing with an invisible opponent and her internal dialogues?

Why had she run away, back at the pottery studio? It was perfectly rational for her to be scared of Alberto. Alberto belonged to a world different from hers. She was on her way to Princeton, medical school. Alberto wanted to spend his life working with clay.

If it all makes absolute sense, why do I feel like a total jerk?

Grace stared at the woman banging her head softly on the table. Out the window, she saw that it had started to rain. She wondered how Alberto would make it back home in the rain.

• •

The women who had been working at the table behind Alberto and Grace were now standing in front of the studio's window watching rain fall in solid sheets of water. Of all the jobs Alberto had to perform at Artes Ticul, the one he loved doing the most was going to the nearby jungle to collect wood for Oxol, the huge cement-and-brick oven where all the clay objects made by him and by Don Andrés were fired and hardened. Oxol was the name they gave to the hungry beast that consumed three truckloads of wood for a firing that lasted two days to burn. It was only fired up once a month. Don Andrés dropped Alberto on the outskirts of Ticul with a gas-powered saw just as the sun was coming up, and Alberto spent the day cutting and collecting wood. Don Andrés had a permit from the state of Yucatán to take all the wood he wanted as long as it was dead wood lying on the ground. Alberto gathered the wood near the main road, and Don Andrés would come by with his truck at dusk. The mosquitoes were so bad that Alberto had to wear a hat with netting, like the kind beekeepers use. It was a job that demanded all his attention or else he'd saw off a hand or pick up a brown viper by mistake. But the best part of wood gathering was getting caught in a storm and hearing the rain pelt the tops of the trees but barely reach him on the ground.

When Alberto finished making the lid for the jewelry box, he put the box and Grace's bowl on a piece of waxed paper so that they would not stick when lifted. He wanted to make Grace a vase with a small opening for a single flower, but the rain was picking up and he had a good hour's walk ahead of him. There was a subway entrance nearby and he could take the number 3 or 5 to the last stop on Flatbush Avenue, but Alberto never took the subway if he could walk there in less than an hour. In the underground tunnels of the subway, he felt as if he had been buried alive. It was on the number 5 train coming home from a painting job that he'd first heard the voice.

Alberto watched the rain. "Gracias," he whispered to himself. He didn't know exactly who he was thanking, but he was grateful that the voice had not spoken to him since he'd entered the studio with Grace. Maybe it was the closeness he had felt with Grace that silenced the voice. It was as if a powerful melody had kept the sound of the voice from reaching him. The feeling he had while he was with Grace was like being with someone you've known since childhood. Well, it was mostly like that. There was also a tingling, a sweet excitement, that he could not deny. Her brown hair, the warmth in her dark eyes, reminded him of home. That closeness and excitement had probably kept the voice away, but Alberto knew that it would return.

He decided right then that he would give the voice a name. A name would make the voice less frightening, and he would be able to stand up to it with greater strength. Alberto remembered talking to Grace about the comic book that Mr. Ramsey had given him. Captain America. That's what he would call the voice. The voice was like the comic book character. It was not real. It had no power over him.

Alberto gave the jewelry box and the bowl to Carol and asked if she would place them in the kiln for him. He would come back next week and glaze them.

"This is beautiful," Carol said, holding up the jewelry box.

"This is more." Alberto pointed to Grace's bowl.

Carol grinned. "The girl that was with you—your girlfriend?"

Alberto felt himself blush. "Oh, no, she's just a friend."

He said goodbye to the women by the window, stepped into the rain, and was immediately soaked. The rain was not the warm rain of home but, as in Ticul, the sensation of being inside torrential water was just as exhilarating.

He turned his face heavenward and drank.

Grace found the stairwell that led to the second-floor balcony before answering her phone. It was her father calling, and part of her wanted to turn the phone off, but not talking to her father would only delay the inevitable. The call would be short.

"Grace!" She detected a note of anxiety in her father's voice, as if he was afraid she'd hang up on him at any moment. "Are you okay? Mom called me and said—"

"I'm fine. I'm a little overwhelmed with schoolwork."

"I can understand that. Grace . . . we should talk . . . about the divorce, the town house . . . I know you're angry with me and this is affecting your studies, your plans for the future, but refusing to talk to me is not the answer."

Grace pulled the cell phone away from her ear. She stared at it for a moment, considered dashing it against the wall, and then placed it back against her ear. "Refusing to talk to you? You mean like you refusing to talk to your father?"

"Where did that come from?"

"A friend mentioned his grandfather today and I thought of Joseph. How long has it been since you talked to him? How long has it been since you saw him? He lives a ten-minute drive from you. You could even walk there."

"That is a totally different situation. It's not comparable."

"No? Explain to me why me not wanting to talk to you is different than you not wanting to talk to your father?"

"It's too complicated to explain on a telephone call. Let's have dinner tonight and chat. Mom said you had an exam tomorrow. We'll make it casual. What do you think?"

"And what about Benny? He's your sister's son. Did you ever make any effort to see him?"

"Grace, let's talk about this over dinner."

"Please, just tell me a little bit of your reasoning behind your separation from them. I need to know."

"What is this? My separation from Joseph and Benny never bothered you before. And, by the way, I send my father money every month. I pay Ernestina's salary, the caregiver that takes care of him and Benny. It's not as if I abandoned them."

Abandon, Grace repeated to herself. What a word! As in banning someone from your life. Like what her father did to her mother, to his father and nephew. Was it that easy to cut yourself off from people you once loved?

"Fine. What did Mom say that made you call me?"

"Michael's mom called her. Something about Michael being distraught over a conversation he had with you this morning. Are you really questioning your decision to go to Princeton in the fall?"

"Distraught? He was distraught?"

"Michael said he saw you walking in the park with the boy who cleaned the windows."

"Oh God! Is that what's worrying everyone?" Grace placed the cell phone against her chest. She could feel the vibrations of her father's voice. All she wanted was a little space to ask what it was she really wanted. And Alberto? Alberto was like a walk in the silence of the park, away from the noisy traffic of her life. "I better go now. I have a test tomorrow."

"Grace, don't hang up!"

Grace pushed a button and her phone went dark.

She went up the stairs and looked down at the reading floor. A small crowd of people had come in to get away from the rain. She went down the stairs, grabbed her things, and walked out into the rain. She made her way through Grand Army Plaza and then headed south on Prospect Park West. She ran for five minutes and then walked. When she got to the pottery studio half an hour later, her shirt was clinging to her chest, her teeth were chattering, and she was shivering. The studio was completely empty, except for Carol, who was fiddling with the knobs on what looked like a microwave. Grace pulled a stool from one of the tables and sat down. All through the rain she had thought of what she would say to Alberto. *I'm sorry I ran off so quickly. If you still want to, you are welcome to bring me the jewelry box and my bowl. Or you can call me when it's done, and I'll come meet you. Here's my phone number. I'd like it if we stayed in touch. Also, I'd like you to have the bowl if you don't find it too ugly.* Those were some of the things she thought of saying. But Alberto was gone, and she felt very alone.

"I had a feeling you might come back," Carol said. "Oh, goodness. Here, let me get you something to dry yourself." Carol went behind the counter and came back with a Native American blanket and wrapped it around

Grace's shoulders. "Alberto left about half an hour ago. Wait a second." The woman picked up a tray with the jewelry box and showed it to Grace. "He made this for you. I haven't fired it up yet so you shouldn't touch it. He said he would return next week to glaze it. I love its simplicity, its beauty."

The jewelry box had a dozen or so flowers carved on its side. The flowers were identical to the ones on the Arita bowl. On the lid there was the unmistakable likeness of a cherry blossom tree. Tears filled Grace's eyes. She wiped them with her wet hand. When Carol returned, Grace asked: "Do you have a phone number where Alberto could be reached?"

"No. Let me think. His sister paid for his studio time. I probably have her phone number somewhere?" Carol looked at Grace again. "Do you live around here?"

"On the other side of the park."

"Well, I think I'm going to close early. No one is going to come in this rain. My car is parked out front. I'll drive you."

"Thank you." Grace opened her backpack and tore a page from her physics notebook. She wrote her name and her cell phone number on it. "If you find his sister's phone number, could you text it to me?"

"Yes, I surely will." Carol took the paper, folded it, and placed it inside a drawer. "I wouldn't worry about Alberto. You will see him again, I'm sure. I have a good nose for romance. I'm never wrong."

Grace blushed. "Oh, no, he's just a friend."

"Mm-hmm. That's what he said."

CHAPTER 7

On Wednesday, Alberto, Lucas, and Jimbo were painting the interior of a brownstone that belonged to Wayne's aunt. Wayne told them they had to finish the job on Monday because he was not making any money on that job. It was Wednesday already, and Wayne was upset it was taking so long. But there was a lot of wood in the house, and wood meant slow going. The aunt was not happy with the delay either. That morning she yelled at Lucas, told him to paint more and talk less. Alberto silently agreed with her. Lucas talked constantly and he had a high-pitched, irritating voice that sounded as if he had inhaled the gas from a balloon.

The name of the woman who owned the house was Mrs. Macpherson, but Lucas called her Mrs. MacBitch. The only time Alberto saw Mrs. Macpherson was when she opened the door for them each morning at eight. With her white bathrobe and long gray hair, she looked like someone who had woken from the dead. After that, she disappeared into her bedroom with a bowl of oatmeal. When they came in the first day, the furniture had already been moved to the center of the room and was covered with brown sheets that smelled of cat litter. All paintings, pictures, and mirrors had been removed from the walls and placed on chairs and sofas and under tables. Alberto could not imagine the old lady doing all that herself. Her arms were thin and brittle. Lucas said the old lady's face was like that of someone who had died and didn't know it.

"She's filthy rich, I guarantee you," Lucas said.

"I don't see nothing but junk in there," Jimbo responded, taking a bite out of a huge sub. They were sitting on the steps outside the brownstone during their lunch break.

"I tell you how I know." Lucas tried to whisper, but his voice came out like a child's squeal. "First day I was here I found an envelope from a company with a funny name. I went home and checked it out on the internet. Turns out it's a company that sells gold coins. She's got them under the mattress. That's where old ladies always hide their valuables."

Take the old lady's money!

Alberto's reprieve from Captain America had been brief. When he got home wet and cold from the pottery studio, Lupe was watching television and holding baby Chato in her arms. She tried to keep the right side of her face away from him, but Alberto could see the purple bruise on her cheek. Alberto was filled with anger. If Wayne had been there, he would not have been able to keep himself from hitting him. It was then that Captain America returned.

Kill him!

Lupe was acting as if she was back on drugs, and that worried Alberto more than Captain America. Last night after baby Chato fell asleep, she grabbed a coat and a purse and told Alberto she had to do an errand. She left and did not come back until after midnight, when Alberto heard her stumble into her room.

"Hey, bozo! Has Wayne ever said anything about his aunt?" Lucas shouted.

Hey, bozo! Loudmouth is talking to you!

"No," Alberto said. He was talking to Captain America and answering Lucas's question. Bozo was just one of many names Lucas used on him. There was also mojado, pendejo, marica, puto, and culero. What did he care what Lucas called him? Captain America was right about one thing: Lucas was a loudmouth. Even when he sounded smart, he was a loudmouth.

"Hey!" Alberto did not turn to look up at Lucas sitting a couple of steps above him. Lucas continued regardless. "You know Wayne has a wife and kids in White Plains. Your sister's wasting her time with him. I've met his wife and she's an ugly old hag, but he ain't ever leaving her, I guarantee you."

"Leave him be," Jimbo said to Lucas, "he don't bother you."

Alberto and Jimbo bumped fists. Jimbo was Alberto's one and only friend.

"I just want him to know which end is up," Lucas continued. "Lupe could do better."

Alberto had never heard Lucas refer to his sister by name. He talked as if he knew her.

"You don't know my sister!" Alberto could not hide his growing anger.

Lucas answered, "Oh, I know her all right . . . and she knows me." He took a joint out of his pocket and lit it. He inhaled deeply and blew the smoke in Alberto's direction. Alberto coughed a few times, waved the smoke away.

He remembered that Lucas had gone up to their apartment on a couple of occasions to get assignments from Wayne. Lucas had stared at Lupe and talked to her when Wayne left the room.

Your sister's a whore.

Lucas continued, "Look, I mean no offense. I just know Lupe deserves better than Wayne. She should be with someone who can make her happy . . . the way she needs to be happy." Lucas winked at Jimbo.

"Shut up, man!" Jimbo said. "Why you got to be talking like that?"

"I haven't said one single thing that's not true," Lucas snapped back.

Alberto stood on the bottom step. He pointed at Lucas. "Stay away from her with your drugs."

"Hey, settle down, man. Don't be so touchy. I just wanna help out, dude. Your sister's not happy."

"Don't pay attention to him." Jimbo rose slowly and placed himself between Alberto and Lucas.

Lucas grinned and continued smoking. Alberto folded the paper bag where Lupe had packed his lunch. He opened and closed his hands twenty times.

You're not a man. You're a worm.

"What does she do in her room all day?" It took Alberto a few moments to understand that Lucas was talking about Mrs. Macpherson and not about Lupe.

"What you hear when you put your damn ear against her door?" Jimbo asked.

"TV noise. She sleeps every day from twelve to three, 'cause two days in a row I heard her snore at that time."

"You been paying lots of attention to the old lady's business," Jimbo remarked.

"Her door's not locked, man. I checked yesterday. I opened the door a crack when I heard her snoring. She's got all kinds of silver stuff all around her room. One big old silver candlestick right next to her bed. We could just go in and take whatever we want."

Jimbo shouted: "Damn, man! What the . . ." Alberto sensed movement behind him. When he turned, Jimbo was standing, his black lunch box dangling from his hand. "You wanna get us fired?"

"Shhh." Lucas had a finger over his lips. "Take it easy."

"Easy is what I be," Jimbo sang. "Come on, let's get back to work."

They went back inside. Lucas and Jimbo continued to argue. It wasn't the first time Lucas had wanted to steal from the places they painted, but Jimbo had always talked him out of it. If things went missing after they painted a place, how hard would it be to figure out who took them? Both Lucas and Jimbo had spent time in prison, but Jimbo wanted a clean life.

Steal the old lady's money.

"No!"

Steal Wayne's money.

Captain America was referring to the cash that Wayne had in a small safe in Lupe's bedroom closet. Lupe, while going through Wayne's wallet, had found the combination to the safe. She had written the six numbers down and hidden the paper inside one of her shoes. One day, when Wayne wasn't there, she opened the safe and showed Alberto the contents. There was a manila envelope bulging with one-hundred-dollar bills.

"Forty thousand dollars," Lupe told him. "I counted it. If something ever happens to me, you get this money and take Chatito to Mexico."

Inside the safe, there was also a sleek black pistol, a box of ammunition, and the Captain America comic book that Wayne had taken from Alberto.

"That belongs to me," Alberto said.

"If you take it, Wayne will know that we opened the safe."

"Why does he keep the comic book in here."

"He says the comic book's probably worth a couple of hundred dollars."

"And the money and the pistol?"

"His safety net, is what he told me."

"Wayne is bad for you," Alberto told Lupe. "You should leave him." How many times had he said that to her? He had lost count.

Wayne is smart. You're not.

Alberto had stopped looking around whenever Captain America spoke. What he could not manage to do was stop listening to him. If there was only a way to turn him off, especially when other people were talking to him or when he needed to sleep. The only thing that seemed to work was concentrating on something else. That's why Alberto preferred painting trims and windowsills rather than walls and ceilings—because he had to pay close attention to the brushstrokes.

Steal and you'll be free.

There was so much wood in these old houses. Alberto liked painting wood with an oil-based stain. He wore a mask to keep the fumes out of his lungs as much as possible. Be free. What did that mean? Free of his duty to Lupe and Chato and his family back home? They were not a burden. They were the reason why he worked and lived.

They're a bag of mierda around your neck.

"*You* are the bag of mierda."

You're chained to them. Slave! Slave!

"I'm chained to you. Why don't you leave me alone?"

I'm sticking around to kill you!

Alberto thought of Grace. Thinking of her was like turning on a light in a dark room. Someone smart had been nice to him. She was shy and a little nervous when she spoke to him. Imagine that. Someday, maybe next Sunday, he would finish the jewelry box. He'd leave the jewelry box at the studio like Grace had asked and maybe put his cell number inside it. If she called and they saw each other, would he ever tell Grace about Captain America? He felt so alone. But telling her would scare her. And what if a day came when he could not resist doing or saying what Captain America commanded?

The sad truth was that he needed to stay away from Grace. Still, it made him happy to know that a girl like Grace had spoken to him like a regular person.

Good riddance.

The strange thing about Captain America was how he used words that Alberto had never heard before. *Maggot. Riddance.* He didn't speak like that. If Captain America was in his brain, why didn't he ever speak to him in Spanish?

"Hablas español, Capitan América?"

You're in the United States, wetback!

Alberto was kneeling on the floor painting the baseboard of the room when he felt a hand shaking his shoulder. It was Lucas standing over him, moving his legs nervously as if he needed to go to the bathroom.

"Hey. We gotta go. Jimbo's got an emergency at home. His mom. I'll call Wayne on my way there. We'll make up the hours tomorrow. You stay and finish the wood. Lock up."

Alberto stood. Jimbo came out from the back carrying his lunch box. He walked past Alberto and Lucas without saying anything or looking at them.

"He's worried about his old lady," Lucas said. "Hey, I

apologize about what I said about Lupe out there on the steps. I was out of line. Got to go now."

Lucas picked up the large, red canvas bag where they carried brushes and other painting tools and hurried out the door. Alberto put the brush on top of the can and went to the back rooms. The bedroom where Lucas and Jimbo had been working was almost finished. Lucas, or more likely Jimbo, had placed rollers and brushes in a bucket of water. Alberto walked out of the room and inspected the remaining bedroom and bathroom. Everything was in order. The door to Mrs. Macpherson's room was closed. Alberto could hear people talking on the television.

Open the door. Steal the gold.

Alberto grabbed the door's round knob before he realized what he was doing. Was he obeying Captain America's commands now? He quickly drew his hand away from the doorknob, went back to the living room, and continued painting the baseboard.

Take her money! She doesn't need it. You do.

"No." Alberto was dizzy. Maybe from paint fumes. Maybe from resisting Captain America's commands. But he had to admit, money would make things easier for him and his family. Seven dollars an hour was not very much. What was happening to him? Four days ago, he was content. Captain America's words were dripping poison into his thoughts.

Stealing is okay. She doesn't need the money.

Alberto's father was a ladrón de luz. That's what the CFE, the Comisión Federal de Electricidad, called a person who illegally connected houses to their grid. Where did his father learn to do that? Alberto didn't know. If the CFE ever discovered the identity of the ladrón de luz, they would put him in jail. The people his father helped by giving them electricity did not call his father a thief.

He was a criminal.

Alberto closed his eyes. He was suddenly bone tired. The marrow in his bones ached.

Kill her. Kill her. Kill her.

He covered his ears with the palms of his hands. If he could only sleep. Even ten minutes would be good. Sleep was like the Lago Esmeralda back home. A lake deep and cool. Underneath its dark green surface, no sound, no voice could penetrate. Alberto let himself slowly sink to the bottom. He sank slowly as if he were floating, down, down into the silence.

There were images. An old woman who had fallen

asleep sitting up in bed with her mouth open. A half-full bowl of oatmeal on the nightstand. A tattered white nightgown. Long gray hair falling over the woman's chest. The sudden look of terror on the pallid face. A thread of blood streaming down her cheek.

Alberto opened his eyes. His T-shirt was soaked with perspiration. His heart was racing. He stood and went to the bathroom. There was a small bottle of dish soap and a roll of paper towels by the sink. Mrs. Macpherson had left that out for them. His hands were sticky. That was strange. He never got paint on himself. When he got out of the bathroom, he noticed that the door to the old lady's bedroom was slightly open. Fear gripped him.

You killed her.

He leaned closer to the door. The TV was on. He heard labored breathing—like when his father kept everyone awake. He moved away from the door quickly and quietly and almost ran back to the living room. He must have fallen asleep momentarily and had a dream. He stuck his hands through an opening in his painter's overalls and took out his cell phone. It was a quarter to five. He saw that he had finished painting the baseboard on the living room floor. He did not remember doing it. It was good when time at work sped by like that. He closed the can of paint, cleaned the brush in the kitchen sink, and then cleaned the sink. He stepped outside and waited for Captain America to speak.

Silence.

"Good," Alberto said. "Give it a rest. You've talked enough for one day."

CHAPTER 8

Grace dropped her backpack by the door and headed for the sofa. She stretched herself out and then used her feet to kick her shoes off. She regretted going to school. She should have listened to her mother and stayed home another day. The day after she walked to the pottery studio, she'd woken up with a fever of 102 degrees. Her mother called Grace's school and told them she would not be able to take the physics test scheduled for that morning. A makeup exam was arranged for the following Monday.

Grace stayed home on Monday and Tuesday, and Miriam stayed home as well, even though the crisis in the office with Lenny was still raging. Not once during those two days they were together did her mother say anything about the events of Sunday. Not one question about Grace's conversation with her father. Yet, even though nothing was spoken, Grace could see the concern in her mother's eyes. Her mother was seeing something in Grace that she had never seen before.

When Grace returned to school on Wednesday, Michael acted as if she were mortally ill. He touched her forehead and brought her a cup of hot chocolate during lunch and behaved as if their conversation on Sunday was perfectly understandable now that he knew she'd been getting sick. The only difference to their routine was that he did not offer to drive her home after school.

Now, lying on the sofa, Grace remembered the conversation with Stella earlier that afternoon. Grace had been walking home after school when Stella caught up with her. Grace was glad to see her best friend even though she had looked forward to walking home alone. Grace also felt guilty for not responding to Stella's calls and texts. Stella was bubbly and caring but also relentlessly nosy. She would not settle for "I don't know" when that's all that Grace could offer.

"Grace, wait, what's going on? I've been trying to get ahold of you for three days. I called you Monday and all day yesterday and today the only time I saw you was at lunchtime. You were talking to Michael and I didn't want to interrupt."

"I got hit with the flu, I think."

"You're pale." Stella put her hand on Grace's cheek.

"My legs feel like they're full of lead. So does the inside of my head."

"You shouldn't be walking home. I'll call a car."

"No, please. I want to walk. I'm sorry I didn't call you back. I've been so out of it."

"Here." Stella unstrapped the backpack from Grace's back using only her right hand. "I'll carry this. I can only go with you part of the way. I'm headed over to PT."

"I'm so self-absorbed these days. I didn't even ask you about your arm."

"A month or two of physical therapy and I'll be as good as a ninety-year-old lady. You're going to have to get a new partner for doubles."

"I'm so sorry."

"It's not so bad. I'm making the most of it." Stella lifted the black sling that held her left arm. Then she said in a serious tone, "So, what is really going on with you? It's not just the flu, is it? I'm your best friend, remember?"

"You sound hurt. You're hurt because you think I've frozen you out. Don't be hurt, please. I seem to be questioning things."

"It's okay. But you need to talk to me. Give me some details. What exactly are you questioning? Michael? Princeton? Medical school?"

Grace stopped walking. She looked away from Stella's piercing eyes.

"Oh my God!" Stella stopped suddenly in the middle of the sidewalk. "Oh my God! I had no idea. Did I miss something? How was it that I did not see this coming? Is this serious?"

Grace started walking. She thought of the doodles she had been making in her physics notebook. Circles and squares. Circles within squares. Squares inside circles. Doodles and not words were what filled her brain. "I don't know. I don't know. Is the questioning serious? Yes, it feels serious, but not in a terribly bad way. I don't know how to describe what this questioning is exactly. It's as if I were walking happily and then it occurred to me to look down and I saw that I was on a tightrope fifty feet up in the air. That's not exactly it either. It's like I'm missing a good reason to do all the stuff that seemed so important a week ago. Am I making any sense?"

They reached the end of the street and waited for the walk sign. When it came, Stella said, "Did you meet a guy? Someone you find kind of exciting?"

"What? Why would you ask me that?"

"Okay, don't be mad at me. On Monday, Michael caught up with me on the way to the cafeteria and he asked if I noticed anything different about you. I said no. He said something about you and a handsome Latino walking together in the park."

"Alberto," Grace said, shaking her head. "He came to clean our windows and then we walked together. He was very nice, but he's not responsible for my current mental confusion." The light changed and they walked. Stella kept looking at Grace.

"What?" Grace finally asked.

"I haven't seen your cheeks turn bright red since Arnie Roth gave you a white rose in seventh grade."

"Okay, maybe my heart did go pitter-patter a little. Mostly it was eye-opening to talk to him. He was, I don't know, so real."

"Real. As opposed to . . ."

Grace continued talking, animated now. "Alberto was a very, very nice guy. He made me think about things I hadn't thought about in a long time. Do you know that I have a grandfather and cousin that live a half-hour walk from us, but I haven't seen or talked to them in four years?"

"You mentioned them, but you never told me the full story."

"I don't know the full story. Bits and pieces. What matters is that there's a little boy out there who is being raised by a blind old man and a housekeeper and I never gave it a second thought."

"Grace, don't be so hard on yourself. There's only so many things we can give second thoughts to. Well, looks like this is my corner. PT's that way." Stella pointed to a side street. Stella hesitated and then asked mischievously, "So how hot was this Alberto boy really? On a scale of one to ten."

"Twelve. Maybe thirteen." Grace tried to joke, but her words came out full of sadness.

"Grace." Stella grabbed Grace's hand. "Maybe you should talk to someone."

"I'm talking to you, my best friend."

"I mean someone professional. Remember the doctor in Sunset Park I saw when I was having eating issues? Not that I still don't have them." Stella grabbed her chubby cheek and pulled it.

Grace smiled. "You're perfect." She was silent for a moment and then she said softly, "This questioning doesn't feel like an illness."

Stella hugged Grace with her one good arm. "I'm just worried about you."

"I know, I know. I'll be all right."

"Can your best friend give you some unsolicited advice?"

"Please."

"Don't make any decisions right now. About whatever. If you want to see the hot boy that makes you *think*, see him, but keep all the balls you're currently juggling in the air. That didn't sound right, but you know what I mean. Keep coming to school even if your mind is not there. Respond to messages and texts from your friends. Don't make anything final, not yet. Do you understand what I'm saying?"

"Keep all the balls I'm currently juggling in the air. I'll write that down as soon as I get home. Heck, I don't think I need to write that down. Those words are embedded here forever." Grace touched her temple first and then her heart.

Now, as she lay on the sofa, Grace remembered what she had said to Stella about how her grandfather and her cousin Benny lived half an hour away but in a different world. Why had she never tried to enter that other world? Who or what had stopped her? Her father's dislike for what he called the "delusional hocus-pocus of religion"? Why was her aunt Deborah so determined that Benny grow up in that world? Did her grandfather and Benny have something that maybe she needed now?

She rose quickly and walked over to her backpack. She took out her cell phone and looked up a number in her contacts.

"Hello." It was a woman's voice.

"Hi, this is Grace. Is this Ernestina?" Grace guessed it was the woman who took care of Joseph and Benny.

"Yes, Dios mío! What a nice surprise!"

"You know who I am?"

"Of course I do! Joseph talks about you all the time. He and Benny just stepped out. They went for their walk around the block. I'm glad I answered his phone."

"Oh. I can call back later."

"I'm so sad that he's not here. Hearing you will

make him so happy. Why you never call before? Or come over?"

"I've been asking myself that. I'm not sure."

"Well, I think I know. You tell your father holding on to that kind of bitterness is not good for his health. Joseph is a stubborn old man too. Like father, like son."

Yes, Grace thought, stubborn was one way to describe her father. "Ernestina, can I ask you something?"

"Of course you can."

"What really happened between my father and Joseph?"

"Ay Dios mío! Why do you want to hear that sad story again?"

"I don't know if I ever heard the details."

"What did your father tell you?"

"Not very much. That after Aunt Deborah died, Joseph refused to let Benny come live with us."

Grace heard a deep sigh. "Let me sit down." When Ernestina spoke again, there was a tired tone to her voice. "Well, when your aunt Deborah was sick, your father wanted Benny to come live with him when the time came, with all of you. Do you remember? You were excited about having a little brother."

Ernestina was right. She had been excited at the

prospect of Benny coming to live with them. She'd been fourteen—only four years ago—how was it that she had never shown any interest in Benny after that?

Ernestina continued, her breathing becoming deeper and more rapid. "Just before she died, Deborah made Joseph Benny's guardian. When she was in the hospital dying of cancer, your aunt decided she wanted Benny to grow up with a religious education. She knew your father would not do that on account of your father was very against all religion. Is he still that way?"

"Very much so."

"But why he should object so much to Benny growing up religious, I don't know. Joseph, the poor soul, doesn't understand either. It's not like he was going to train Benny to be a witch. That boy is an angel, let me tell you. I hope you can come see him someday. So, where was I with the story?"

"My father didn't want Benny to live with Joseph."

"Yes, he felt very strong about that. He argued and argued with Joseph. It gets so bad that your father hires a lawyer to fight Joseph's guardianship. That's when it gets very ugly. But the judge decided to honor your aunt Deborah's wishes."

Grace was silent. Ernestina was right. It was a sad

story. But there was also something that seemed wasteful. So much time wasted. Time she could have spent with Benny and Joseph. Grace took a deep breath and asked, "And Benny? Does he like school?"

"Oh, yes! He loves school. It's a Jewish school, like your aunt wanted. You know Joseph was never religious. He returned to being a Jew after your aunt died, for Benny's sake. He's trying. He even goes to synagogue with Benny, now and then."

"Thank you, Ernestina. This has been helpful to me."

"I'll text you my phone number. This phone is always getting lost. Joseph will be so happy you called. And Benny too. Joseph talks to him about you, you know. He tells him that you are his only cousin. I wish you would come visit."

"Yes," Grace said, "I'm going to try. Bye, Ernestina."

"Bye, child."

Grace walked over to the living room windows. The image of eight-year-old Benny came to her. He had stayed with them in their town house during Aunt Deborah's last days. He liked to read books about the universe, how stars were born and how they died. He helped Grace paste luminescent stars on the ceiling of her bedroom in the form of the constellation Leo. The day his mother died, Benny hid himself. It was Grace who found him in her closet. They lay on her bed side by side looking up at Leo. Then Joseph came to get him and not once had she tried to get in touch with him. Hard as she tried, she could not understand that about herself. She looked out at the park and found the tree with purple-pinkish flowers. She had looked up its name when she was home sick. It was a redbud—a name that did not jibe with the color of its flowers. Now, looking at it, the redbud tree resembled something she wanted to make or be, but did not know how.

CHAPTER 9

It was a long walk from Bay Ridge, where Mrs. Macpherson's apartment was located, to Flatbush, where Alberto lived with Lupe. This was one of those times when he should have taken a bus, but after a whole day on his knees, he needed to move. The walk was peaceful for the first hour and then Captain America began to pester him about the need to steal Wayne's money from the safe. There was a new, urgent tone to Captain America's voice that was difficult to ignore. Alberto hoped that holding baby Chato in his arms would quiet Captain America.

Lupe was not home when Alberto arrived two hours later. It was strange for Lupe not to be home at seven. There was nothing on the stove, and the sink was full of breakfast dishes. Baby Chato's stroller was by the door.

She's out getting high.

Alberto checked in Lupe's bedroom. The only thing that seemed to be missing was baby Chato's diaper bag. Lupe must have gone out with baby Chato to get take-out for dinner.

She abandoned you.

Alberto opened the closet and saw Lupe's brown suitcase on the top shelf. He exhaled with relief. Why did he listen to Captain America? Because he sounded as if he knew everything? But he didn't.

He flopped down on his bed and tapped Lupe's number on his cell phone.

"Where are you?" It was Wayne.

"Here. Where's Lupe?"

"She's with me. She's busy changing the baby. You at the apartment?"

"Yes."

Alberto heard voices in the background, then a beat, like a heartbeat. Wayne must have been talking to someone while he held the phone against his chest.

"Hey, Alberto." Wayne sounded nice for the first time ever. "I need you to stay where you are. I'll be over with Lupe in about fifteen minutes. Have you eaten?"

"No."

"Okay, we'll go out and get something to eat when we get there, maybe Mexican. Okay? Just stay there, don't go anywhere."

"Is everything all right?"

"Yeah, sure. Be there soon. Don't go anywhere."

Alberto dropped the phone on the bed. Something was not right. Wayne was never nice to him.

Grab the money!

Alberto took his shirt off and dropped it in the small washing machine by the kitchen. He went back to his room and was looking for clean pants when he heard the ping in his phone indicating a text message. He read the message from Lupe:

The police are coming for you. They found out you killed Wayne's aunt. Run. Get your money. Now. Throw away your phone.

A wave of panic went through him. He could not believe the words he'd read. He stood there unable to move. The image of his father getting electrocuted came to Alberto. His father had climbed up an electric pole to connect a neighbor's house to the electrical grid. A group of people watched and cheered. Alberto saw a flash of white light and sparks, his father falling backward to the ground, smoke coming out of his hands.

You killed the old woman!

Alberto's legs would not move. His feet were stuck in the quicksand of one question: Did he kill Mrs. Macpherson?

He did not remember doing it. Unless that dream was real. What really happened? There had been a sticky substance on his hands. He thought it was paint, but it could have been blood. Alberto placed his hand on his forehead, remembering. The door to the old woman's room was slightly open. There was gasping. The last sounds of someone dying?

Damn right you killed her!

Alberto took one step and then another. He stuck his cell phone in his pocket and walked out of his room, his head spinning. He stood outside Lupe's bedroom and waited for his heart to resume a slower beat. In the past he had been able to overcome fear by slowing down deliberately. After a few moments, his head cleared enough for him to act. He remembered that Lupe had said "your money." She meant the money he gave her to send home to his mother.

Take Wayne's money.

Lupe kept Alberto's money in the drawer by her bed in a white envelope. Alberto took the envelope and stuck it in his pocket. He went back to his room and stuffed some clothes in his backpack. He took one last look at the high school equivalency books on his desk and then walked out. A few seconds later he returned, put a clean T-shirt on, and grabbed the picture of his family.

Take the money and the gun.

He was out of the apartment building when he saw the police cars at the other end of the street. They did not have their sirens on and were not speeding. Alberto crossed the street and found a place behind the staircase where he could observe.

Get rid of the phone!

Alberto dropped his cell phone and stomped on it until crystal and plastic scattered on the sidewalk. Since when did he start listening to Captain America?

I told you to kill the old bag and you did it.

"No, I didn't."

You did. I told you to do it.

"I don't do what you say."

He looked around to make sure no one had heard him and then he picked up the pieces of broken phone and threw them in a garbage can. There were three police cars. They parked in front of his building and four policemen went up.

A force pushed him toward the police car to turn himself in. It was the right thing to do if he was guilty. But there were doubts in his mind about whether he had killed Mrs. Macpherson. Why would he kill her? It was not in him to do something like that. Because Captain America asked him to do it? He would never obey a command like that. He was still in control.

You killed her.

Two policemen who'd stayed behind began to walk in his direction. Alberto moved slowly away. Where to? His eyes got blurry. He fought back tears. Where to? There was no place to go. What friends did he have? Chatito was his best friend. Jimbo? But he could not remember where Jimbo lived. What about Grace? Was she a friend? No, he could not trouble her life. He was alone.

How much money you got?

Alberto took out the envelope from his back pocket and counted the money. One hundred and ninety-five dollars. There should have been more. Every week he gave Lupe two hundred and eighty dollars. That was what eight hours of work five days a week at seven dollars an hour came to. Lupe gave him forty for him to spend as he wished. She sent five hundred to Ticul every month. Where was the rest?

She snorted your money!

Maybe Lupe put the rest of the money in the bank. It would be safer there.

And maybe someday you'll graduate from high school!

Lupe was addicted to heroin when she worked at the nightclub. But she checked herself into a rehab place when she found out she was pregnant with baby Chato. Wayne paid for the rehab. Paying for Lupe's rehab had given Alberto hope that Wayne was a good person.

Your sister is a leech, like you.

Alberto kept walking without direction until he found himself in front of the Brooklyn College library. It was dark now, and the lights around the campus had gone on. The grounds of the college had always seemed safe and restful. He liked how the students simply assumed that he was one of them. One day, he thought, his sister Mercedes would study in a place like this.

Alberto sat on a bench near the entrance of the library.

He was suddenly exhausted, drained. He needed sleep but he was afraid of closing his eyes. He noticed that despite everything, he was hungry. He saw students carrying bags of food and so he walked in the direction they were coming from. On one of the streets adjacent to the college he saw a row of food trucks. He bought two tacos and a drink from one of them.

Alberto took his food and sat on the grass opposite the library. He looked at the food in the bag and placed it next to him. He couldn't bring himself to eat. It was dark now and he needed to find a place to spend the night. When he and Lupe had first come from Mexico, they stayed in an apartment in the Bronx with a woman who liked to be called "Daisy," but whose real name was Esperanza. For a fee of one thousand dollars, Daisy wrote a letter saying that she was their aunt and would vouch for their return to Mexico. Based on that letter, he and Lupe got a one-month visitor's visa. A couple of weeks after they arrived, Lupe and Daisy got in a fight over money that Daisy thought Lupe had stolen from her. Daisy kicked them out and they moved to an ugly and smelly hotel. Then Alberto got a job with a moving company while Lupe started dancing in a nightclub.

She's a leech and a whore.

Between the two of them, they made enough to move into a tiny apartment with Pilar, one of the girls at the nightclub. They all lived there for three months until, again, there was a fight between Pilar and Lupe. Alberto never found out what the fight was about, but by then Wayne was in the picture and he provided them with a place to live.

You and your sister are garbage.

Lupe was no saint, Alberto recognized that. There had been problems in Ticul. Staying out all night long. How many times had his father gone out looking for her? Alberto remembered his mother's words as they waited for the bus that would take them to the airport in Mérida.

"Cuídala mucho."

Had Alberto done all he could to take care of her? He pleaded with her not to work in that nightclub, but how could he stop her? They needed the money she made to survive. His salary moving furniture was not enough to pay the rent, even in the most run-down apartments. When Lupe got pregnant with baby Chato, she changed. She gave up her cigarettes. There was that awful, hellish three weeks in rehab when Lupe detoxified herself. He came to see her every day after work. The rehab place was a building in Long Island that looked like any other run-down four-story apartment building. The linoleum floors smelled of ammonia and vomit.

She got pregnant to hook Wayne.

"Shut up! She's my sister!"

Alberto waited for a response and when none came, he stood and walked out to the street, where the food trucks were still vending. He walked fast as if someone was waiting for him somewhere out there and he was late. In fact, there was no one waiting for him, and he was not walking anywhere in particular. His father had taught him to face fear. He was trying to do that, but how could he face the fear of losing his mind when he needed his mind to do it? What if Captain America had taken over his mind momentarily and he'd killed a human being?

You killed her. Have I ever lied to you?

"You're not real. You don't tell the truth. I'll find out if I really killed her."

That was the thread he must follow now. The search for the truth. The only thread that could keep him from getting totally lost.

CHAPTER 10

Alberto stepped into a drugstore near Brooklyn College and bought a prepaid phone. He walked nine blocks back to Lupe's apartment and stood on the corner of the street watching. Wayne's SUV was not there and there were no police cars. He was about to walk down the street when he saw movement inside a car parked in front of the building. He had never seen the car before.

You're a wanted criminal.

Alberto could see the light in his room. Someone had gone in there and forgot to turn it off. Lupe would be home by herself now. Who was going to help her with baby Chato? Alberto held the new cell phone in front of him. The only numbers he knew by memory were Lupe's and the number of Mercedes's cell phone in Ticul. He called Mercedes every Sunday at four p.m. so he could talk to his mother and Chela. Could he call this Sunday? He would need to find out how to make international calls on the prepaid phone.

He dialed Lupe's number and then ended the call before the first ring. What if the police were listening to Lupe's phone? He wished he had memorized Jimbo's phone number. He remembered now that Jimbo lived in Brownsville. His mother worked in a church near their apartment. Jimbo's last name was the name of a flower. Not Rose or Daisy or Lily. An unusual flower. He couldn't remember. His head wasn't working right.

You think?

Even if he knew Jimbo's last name, what good would it do? How would he find him? In Ticul they had a phone book thin as a comic book, but here in Brooklyn? He had never seen one. Jimbo told him working in a church was the perfect job for his mother. She liked to pray while she worked. Jimbo was nice to him. He'd taught Alberto how to bowl.

Tomorrow he would walk to Brownsville and look for Jimbo's mother, who could get him to Jimbo. How many churches could there be in Brownsville?

Jimbo hates you.

One time he went with Jimbo and his girlfriend to Coney Island, and he and Jimbo went on the roller coaster but Gloria, that was the name of Jimbo's girlfriend, refused to get on. Jasmine, that was Jimbo's last name, Alberto remembered. Lucas teased him about his name. "You smell so hot, Jasminee," he'd say to Jimbo.

Jimbo would correct him. "Jasmeen, not Jasminee."

Jimbo Jasmine would help him find out if he'd killed Mrs. Macpherson. Jimbo would hide him from the police.

You know what happened.

"Jimbo will know what to do."

You killed someone. No one wants anything to do with you.

Alberto decided to call Lupe. He didn't care if the police were listening. Why did the police think he did it? What did the police tell Lupe? If it was clear that he killed the woman, then he would walk up to the car in front of Lupe's building and turn himself in.

You're dumb as nails.

"Please!" Alberto pleaded. "I need calm to think." It

took all his strength to ignore Captain America, and he felt himself getting weaker and weaker. His mind was like a flashlight when the batteries are dying. Alberto tapped Lupe's number. On the fifth ring, she answered.

"Yes, who's this?"

"It's me."

"Alberto . . . are you okay?"

"I'm okay."

"No se puede hablar." Lupe sounded scared. Alberto couldn't tell whether it was because the police might be listening or because she believed he was a killer.

"I need to know. Why do they think I killed Mrs. Macpherson?"

Lupe was silent and then the words came out in a nervous rush. "Lucas said she was alive when they left at two. Wayne's aunt called him at five. She could barely talk. I was with Wayne when she called. When we got there she was still warm. Her head bashed in. I saw her. It was horrible!" A sound like a sob came out of Lupe.

"Bashed?" Alberto had not heard the word before, but it sounded evil. Was he capable of that?

"Cracked. Tenía la cabeza destrozada." There was a tone of both disbelief and accusation in Lupe's voice. Alberto heard her take two deep breaths and knew she was trying very hard not to say what she wanted to say. When she spoke, her words sounded as if they were coming from a stranger. "It's better if you don't run anymore. Her silver candlesticks and gold coins are gone. The police found blood on the shirt you were wearing. They found the shirt in the washing machine. They're testing it but they're pretty sure it's the woman's blood."

"I . . . don't remember."

"The police also know you took Wayne's money . . . in the safe. The gun also."

"No! I only took my money. The money I gave you."

"I'm only telling you the police know you did it."

Lupe's words and tone reminded Alberto of the times when Lupe lied to Papá about where she'd been. "I have to go now." There was nothing more to say. Lupe had stopped believing in him.

"Turn yourself in, that's my advice. It's what's best. Lucas told me he's heard you talking to yourself out loud. Like you're talking to someone. I've heard you too. You don't sleep. I speak to you and you're like someplace else. Maybe you didn't know what you were doing. You can get help if you turn yourself in."

Alberto turned off the cell phone. He began to walk toward Flatbush Avenue, where there were cars and noise and people walking. He turned into an alley and emptied out his backpack. Wayne's money was not in there. Was it possible that he could steal Wayne's money and not know it? Who took it, then? The only other people who knew about the money were Wayne and Lupe.

You took it and hid it.

"I wouldn't do that."

He was responding to Captain America out loud as if he were real. How often had he been doing that without being aware? Lucas had heard him. Was he killing and stealing without knowing as well? He was falling apart. There was no getting around it.

"Estoy loco."

It started to rain. The envelope with his money was still in his pocket. He opened it and counted it. After the tacos and telephone, he was down to one hundred and fifty-five. He took out a ten-dollar bill and stuck it in his pocket. He placed everything else in the backpack. The only place he could think of finding shelter was Prospect Park. The place where he and Grace had walked.

"Grace." Was Grace real or did he imagine her? She gave him a glass of water with ice cubes. He began to run.

The pavilions at the entrance to Prospect Park were

full of homeless people. Most of them were dry, which meant that they had seen the rain coming and gotten out of its way in time. Alberto had not noticed the smell of impending rain. He found a space near the entrance and lowered himself to the ground. The cement was cold and damp. The smell of urine and human sweat filled his nostrils. Alberto had never felt so lonely and so scared in such a crowded, noisy place. People shouted to each other or to no one in particular. The man next to him was arguing about a missing watch with someone.

"You gotta give it back. It's my momma's!"

The man was talking to someone in his head. Alberto tried to gauge his age but couldn't. Somewhere between twenty and fifty. There was no one there his age. No one who didn't look like they had grown accustomed to being uncared for and forgotten. *This is where I belong*, Alberto thought. He closed his eyes for a moment and when he opened them, there was a big man in a raincoat hovering over him, kicking Alberto's leg.

"Hey, kid, you gotta pay the fee! You wanna stay here? Pay the fee!"

Alberto stood slowly. He was tired. The man's breath smelled of the same mouthwash that Wayne used. A mixture of alcohol and mint.

"He took my momma's watch! I seen him do it." The man on the ground pointed at Alberto.

Kick him in the mouth!

"How much?" Alberto asked, reaching for his wallet.

The man's eyes moved between Alberto's face and the wallet. He seemed to be sizing Alberto up. How much of a fight would Alberto put up if he snatched the wallet?

"Show me what you got, and I tell you how much."

Alberto opened his wallet and gave him the ten-dollar bill.

Punch him! Break his nose!

The man grabbed the wallet, looked in there, dropped it on the ground. "What else you got?" The man glanced at the backpack.

"Anything else, you have to fight me." Alberto stared into the man's eyes.

The man stared back, looked up and down at Alberto, and then grinned, nodded, and walked away. Alberto slid back down, picked up his wallet. He stretched out with the backpack under his head.

"My momma got that watch on her fiftieth anniversary," the man next to him said. Alberto didn't know whether the man was talking to him or to his voices.

You are one big coward!

Alberto turned on his side. Between the man with the stolen watch and Captain America, there was not a chance he would sleep. He decided to go over all he could remember from the moment he got up that morning, a lifetime ago, to the last conversation he'd had with Lupe. When he finished, the man next to him was snoring and Captain America seemed to have gotten tired of yelling at him. The rain had tapered off to a steady drizzle. The only light in the pavilion came from the cigarette of the man who had taken Alberto's money. Alberto couldn't be sure, but it seemed as if the man's eyes were fixed on him. Alberto ignored him. In going over the events of the day, Alberto was sure of one thing. No matter what Captain America or anyone else said, he could not bring himself to believe he had killed Mrs. Macpherson. But neither could he bring himself to believe with absolute conviction he had not. Given the choice between those two options, Alberto decided he would choose to believe he was innocent. If he believed he killed the woman, wouldn't that make it easier to yield to Captain America's commands? He needed to believe he was a good person. If the truth was otherwise, then so be it.

Alberto closed his eyes. Then he opened them again. He felt an urge to say a prayer. He could not recall any of the prayers he'd learned in catechism class. That was so long ago, and he had never been interested in church teachings. He could try to make up his own prayer, but he wasn't very good with words. He remembered how he'd felt when making the jewelry box with Grace by his side. It wasn't a prayer, but it was close.

CHAPTER 11

Grace got up from her bed and checked her phone once again. Why did she think that she might have a text from Alberto? He probably wouldn't make it back to the pottery studio until the following Sunday. He wouldn't have her phone number until then. She was opening the window so she could better listen to the rain when she heard her mother say, "What?" She walked out of her bedroom and saw her mother talking to a middle-aged woman dressed in a brown pantsuit. They both turned and watched Grace come down the hall.

"This is Detective Lydell," Miriam said.

Grace extended her hand and barely touched Detective Lydell's. She felt her heart race momentarily. Her mother's face was calm, so it was not about her father. Then what? "What happened? Did something happen?"

"Detective Lydell had some questions about the young man who cleaned our windows." Miriam looked steadily at Grace.

"Alberto?" Grace asked, worried.

Detective Lydell grinned. "Yes. Alberto Bocel. I'm following up with some of the people he saw last Sunday."

"Why?" Grace asked.

"He's a person of interest in a robbery-murder." Detective Lydell waited for Grace's reaction.

"What?" Grace muttered, barely audible.

"We think he murdered the eighty-five-year-old owner of the apartment he was painting and then took her valuables."

Grace froze. She did not move a single muscle of her body. "A person of interest," Grace repeated.

"More like a suspect," Detective Lydell said.

Grace's heart picked up speed again. Everything in her told her that the kind and gentle person who'd made her a jewelry box could not kill anyone. But how well did she know Alberto? She remembered Michael's assessment of Alberto: *He's a little off.* "Are you sure? He seemed like a nice guy." Why did she feel an overwhelming need to protect Alberto from this woman? There was a haughtiness in the way she talked that made Grace dislike her.

"Sure as can be."

Miriam tried to break the tension between Grace and Detective Lydell. "I told the detective the young man cleaned our windows and then left. He did a good job."

The detective waited for Grace to say more. The woman clearly understood that silence made people uncomfortable, made them say more than they should. Grace glanced at Detective Lydell's wedding ring. If there was a human being somewhere inside this person, it was buried deep.

Detective Lydell opened a notepad and read. "Carol Jennings, the owner of the pottery studio, said you were with Bocel on Sunday. You left and then you came back an hour or so later and asked her to give your phone number to Bocel. Has he called you?"

"Do I need to call my lawyer?" Miriam asked.

"It's a simple question, ma'am."

Grace waited for her mom to nod in her direction before responding. "I was with him at the studio for about an hour. Then I went to the library and, yes, I came back and gave the owner my phone number so she could give it to Alberto."

"What was the reason for giving him your phone number?"

Grace looked at her mother briefly. She too seemed interested in the answer to Detective Lydell's question. What was the reason? Grace wished she could give an accurate answer. *Because I felt something I've never felt before when I was with him.* Instead, she said, "So he could call me when the clay bowl I made had been glazed."

"And has he called you or otherwise communicated with you?"

"No," Grace said, a note of regret in her voice. "You can check my phone if you like."

Detective Lydell peered into Grace's eyes.

"That won't be necessary, will it, Detective?" Miriam opened the door and gestured for Detective Lydell to leave.

Detective Lydell and Miriam stared at each other for a few moments, and then Lydell took out a card from her jacket's pocket and tossed it on the kitchen table. "If he calls you, call me. Or, better yet, convince him to come see me. You don't want to be charged with obstructing an investigation. It will ruin your bright future."

"Goodbye, Detective." Miriam watched Detective Lydell enter the elevator before closing and locking the door to the apartment. "Well, that was . . . interesting."

Grace pulled out a chair from the kitchen table and sat down. "I can't believe Alberto would do something like that."

Miriam sat across from Grace and took a sip of water from a glass on the table. "Grace, I have to ask."

"I haven't seen or heard from him, Mom. I was telling the truth." Grace heard her mother exhale. "Really, there's nothing for me to say and nothing for you to worry about." Grace stood, went to the refrigerator, opened it, and then closed it. Alberto had thanked her because she had put ice in his glass. "I don't believe he is capable of doing what that woman said he did."

"People surprise us. Even those we've known for a long time," Miriam said, not hiding her sadness.

"If you had talked to him, you would have trusted him too. It's hard to explain. I felt close to him, like I knew him for years."

"I know. I believe you. Your heart let Alberto in. But

the heart can be wrong." Miriam stood and hugged Grace. "Get some sleep, sweetie."

Grace walked slowly down the hall to her room. She kept her hands on the walls as if she were in a ship being tossed around by an angry sea. She turned off the lights and lay down on her bed. Her left hand fell on her phone. She checked her messages, both afraid and hoping to find one from Alberto. There was only a message from Michael:

> Just a reminder that I'm here. Take all the time you
> need. But come back to me. We are us.

She breathed deeply and then exhaled. She read Michael's words once again. What was she doing opening her heart and letting in Alberto, a stranger? There was no room in there for anyone else besides Michael. She knew who Michael was and who Michael was going to be. She could count on him. That was good. That's what she needed. That's what she wanted. Wasn't it?

CHAPTER 12

Alberto was inside the jewelry box he made for Grace. He wasn't sure whether the jewelry box was big as a mountain or whether he was small as an ant. He had no idea how he'd gotten there or who put him there. There was no way for him to get out on his own. He couldn't reach the lid, and even if he could, how would he lift it? He looked up and saw there was a space between the edge of the box and the lid. That gap was the only source of light and air. Alberto was glad that the jewelry box wasn't perfect. If it had been perfect, he would be in total and absolute darkness and he would suffocate. He held his breath because he heard voices. Two people, on the other side of the lid. Alberto shouted and shouted until his voice gave out. He shouted in Spanish and in English, but no one answered.

Alberto opened his eyes and saw four legs. One pair belonged to the man who had demanded a fee earlier that night and the other pair to a skinny man whose face seemed to have been badly burned.

"Having a bad dream, kid?" the burned man asked. His voice sounded like someone trying hard not to laugh.

Alberto saw one leg move back. The foot of the leg was in an unlaced black boot. Alberto managed to move his face slightly so that the boot struck him on his left ear rather than on his eye. He felt a burning liquid ooze out of his eardrum before the pain exploded. His first thought when he could think again was that this was one way to silence Captain America. Then there was another blow. This one was to his rib cage. A hand grabbed his hair and lifted his head. Alberto reached out to grab his backpack, but the hand holding his hair slammed his head on the concrete floor of the pavilion. He saw a white dot turn into a red circle and then everything went black.

When Alberto opened his eyes again, the man who

had slept next to him was going through his pockets, and his backpack was gone. Alberto tried to push him away, but the pain on his upper abdomen prevented him from moving his arm.

"I'm looking for my momma's watch."

Alberto lay still and let the man do what he had to do. With the right hand, he touched his back pocket. His wallet was gone. His father's driver's license from the state of Yucatán was in there. Alberto had kept it because his father had been so happy when he got it. It meant he could drive one of the brewery's trucks and a raise of two hundred pesos a month.

The man was about to take Alberto's shoes when Alberto asked, "Do the voices ever stop?"

The man looked at Alberto with a look that Alberto could not describe. It was as if humanity had momentarily returned to the man's face. "Hefty and the Torch took your stuff."

"They come here every night?" Alberto sat up with effort. He touched the back of his head and then looked at the blood on the palm of his hand. The blood was sticky, a dark red. It reminded Alberto of when he washed his hands in Mrs. Macpherson's apartment.

"Yeah, for sure, they come here. Most every night."

Alberto didn't care about the money; what he wanted to recover was the picture of his family. But the men who took it wouldn't keep something like that. They probably tossed it someplace nearby. Daylight was coming. The other homeless people in the pavilion were rising, folding their gray blankets. "Help me up, please," Alberto asked the man. "You have to get behind me. Put your arms around my chest and pull me up."

"Give me the shoes."

"I need the shoes," Alberto said with a tone of regret in his voice. The man waited to see what else Alberto could offer. "I got nothing."

"Don't wind it so much. You gonna break it."

Alberto was about to respond, but the man was no longer speaking to him. Alberto scooted away from the wall so the man could get behind him and lift him. He felt the thin arms of the man around him and slowly, with his legs, and with the support of the man, he stood.

"Thank you."

He walked slowly outside. There was a trash can near the pavilion. Alberto looked inside and saw his backpack. He lifted it out and opened it. Everything was gone except for the picture of his family. The glass of the frame was broken. He was broken too, his head, his ribs, his mind. He brought the frame to his chest and held it there for a few seconds. He placed the picture in the backpack and began to walk toward to the cherry blossoms at the entrance of the park. Things were not so bad, all things considered. He was still alive. He had the picture of his family. And he had not heard from Captain America since his head was busted. Maybe Captain America escaped through the crack at the back of his skull.

Alberto found himself by the lake at the other end of the park. He did not know how he got there. He had been thinking about his mother and sisters in Ticul and forgot where he was. There was a smell to the lake in front of him that reminded him of the orégano that his mother grew in their backyard. Alberto sat on one of the curved concrete benches that overlooked the lake. On the other side of the lake was a tall building. He had the impression that he had once been inside that building. Then the image of his mother came to him again. His mother was extremely shy and reserved, unlike his father. She pretended to dislike any external show of affection, but it was impossible for her not to laugh when Alberto picked her up and twirled her around. What would his mother do without the money he sent her? She already worked two jobs: making tortillas in the morning and baskets in the afternoon. Could Lupe find a way to help? Wayne didn't give her much. Would Mercedes and Chela have to quit school to find jobs?

Alberto grabbed his head with both hands. He had no answers to any of these questions. Lucas told him that a person with brains and guts could make a year's salary simply by selling a small sandwich-size bag of heroin. Lucas said if he had a little capital, that's what he would do. He'd buy a kilo and sell it. Then another one. Never more than one. Wayne's money was gone. How? If he was the one who took it, where did he put it? The capital of Yucatán was Mérida. What he needed most of all was someone to help him think. Captain America may have gone, but he left a mess in there.

"Grace!" She lived in that tall building. He raised his hand and waved in case she was watching, then quickly lowered it. "I didn't kill anyone," he said. "I didn't kill anyone. Please believe me."

Oh yeah. You killed her.

Alberto struggled and finally managed to stand up. Where could he go? What refuge was there in this lonely city? He looked up at Grace's building one more time. The window to her room was on the tenth floor. How strange that he could remember that and not remember killing Mrs. Macpherson or taking Wayne's money. He counted the windows on the building until he got to the tenth row. He had a strong urge to knock on Grace's door, to hold on to her. She had put ice in his water. She had made a funny-looking, crooked bowl that was the most beautiful thing he had ever seen. He gripped the straps of his backpack with all his might. Inside was the picture of his family. He held on to the straps because if he let go, he would fall into a deep, dark, and endless pit.

CHAPTER 13

Grace woke up to sunlight streaming through her window. The apartment was silent. She put on a pair of blue jeans and walked out of her room. She peered in her mother's bedroom and saw the bed neatly made. She'd forgotten to set the alarm clock next to her bed and now she had one hour to get to school. She washed her face in the bathroom down the hall and then went back to her room and grabbed her backpack. When she came out, she heard her mother's voice. She was sitting on a kitchen stool, her back to Grace.

"Of course I know his demands are outrageous, but

litigation is not the answer. We pay him and end the mess. Life must go on."

Long silence.

"I will do that."

Miriam placed her cell on the kitchen island and grabbed the sides of her head.

Grace came up behind her and wrapped her arms around her mother. "Mommy, you need a vacation."

"You're up! I was hoping I'd see you before I left. How are you feeling today?"

"Better, I think."

"You look exhausted. Are you sure you're all right?"

"I didn't sleep all that well."

"The visit by the detective. It was . . . disturbing. I know."

Graced poured coffee into a white mug. "Disturbing," she repeated. "But life must go on, no?"

"You're being sarcastic, but yes, life goes on. That young man, Alberto . . . maybe he is guilty, maybe he's not. There's really nothing you can do."

"That sounds so harsh, doesn't it? There's nothing I can do. Why does that make me feel like a coward?"

Miriam peered into her empty cup. "I don't know where that feeling comes from. When we would like to help someone who is drowning but we can't, we just can't, not without us going under ourselves. Oof! Listen to me wax philosophical so early in the morning."

Grace took a long sip of coffee and turned to place the cup in the sink. She turned on the faucet and wiped her eyes.

Miriam stood, turned Grace around, and hugged her. "Sweetie. I know how you feel. Look, if Alberto calls you, tell him we will get a good lawyer for him. We'll help him as best we can, okay?"

"Thank you, Mom. I don't know why everything is affecting me so much these days."

"Grace, maybe it wouldn't hurt to talk to someone about what you've been going through, the doubts about the future you've been having. How you feel about Alberto. I know a really good—"

"Mom, can we talk about this tonight? I want to get to school before classes start and study for the physics test I still need to take."

"Okay, sweetie." Miriam kissed Grace on the cheek and opened the door for her. "Take it easy. I'm worried about you."

"Bye, Mommy."

Grace had just stepped out of the building when her

phone buzzed. It was an unknown number. She never responded to unknown numbers, but maybe it was Alberto.

"Hello?"

"Is this Grace?"

Grace hesitated. The voice of the woman sounded urgent. "Yes."

"I'm Carol, from the pottery studio. Remember me? I gave you a ride to your apartment on Sunday. That big rainstorm."

"Yes, yes. I remember."

"Alberto is here. He's hurt."

"What?"

"Alberto. He's here. I found him leaning against the door to the studio. He was crying uncontrollably. The side of his face is purple, his ear is all mangled up. He's got a gash in the back of his head. He can hardly breathe. A broken rib maybe. I think he may have gotten mugged. He was very disoriented at first but he's better now. I brought him to the room in back of the studio. He doesn't want me to call anyone. A detective woman came by yesterday. I had to give her your address. I don't know if she's contacted you."

"She did."

"Why are the police looking for him? She didn't tell me."

Grace was about to answer Carol's question and then stopped herself. Some instinct told her that telling Carol the truth would make things worse for Alberto and for her. "I don't know. The detective didn't say."

"I can't keep him here. If he's involved in some crime, I could be charged with harboring a criminal. I could lose my business. This is my livelihood. Should I call the police?"

Grace felt a weight descend upon her. Who was Alberto to her? And why was she being put in this position? She was just a teenager trying to get on with her life. She was in the middle of a personal crisis. She had no time for someone else's troubles.

"Grace? Are you there?"

"Yes, I'm here."

"What should I do? Can you come get him? He was calling out your name when I found him."

A very insistent voice in Grace's head was telling her to hang up. What could she do? She barely knew Alberto. He wasn't a friend, not really. He was a stranger. She was attracted to him, but big deal, who wouldn't be? He could be a problem, a load she was not strong enough to bear, a drowning person who would pull her under. But . . . he called her name. He called her.

"I'll come over; maybe I can help."

"Okay. Please hurry."

"Okay." Grace turned the phone off before she could change her mind.

Grace crossed the street and entered the park. She found a path that seemed to cut across and she began to run. She ran because running kept her from thinking. Running was a way to get rid of the fear that threatened to paralyze her or to make her run in the opposite direction. She wished she had not answered her phone. She should have said no when the strange boy asked her to go to the pottery studio with him. She could call Michael now and ask him to pick her up. They could argue about Princeton versus Harvard. But Grace kept running in the direction of Alberto, propelled by—what? Guilt? Maybe. Or maybe that there was someone out there in desperate circumstances who had called her name. Out of all the people in the world, he had called Grace.

The back door to the studio was a steel door that clanged loudly when she knocked. Carol opened on the third knock. Alberto was in a huge, cushiony red armchair in the back of the pottery studio. He was holding a white towel against the side of his face. "Hola!" Grace said, entering the back room. Carol went to the front of the studio and closed the door behind her. She tried to sound chipper, casual. "You look mucho malo."

It made Alberto smile to hear her speak bad Spanish. He grimaced from the pain the smile produced. "It's not so bad."

"No? Where does it hurt?"

Alberto raised the index finger on his right hand. "This is where it doesn't hurt."

Grace didn't laugh or even smile. She looked at the wad of paper towels at the back of his head. "You should go to a hospital."

"No puedo," Alberto said, looking away from Grace.

Grace turned Alberto's head toward her and removed the towel he was holding, flinching at the sight of his face. "Carol said you didn't want her to call anyone. Not even your sister?"

"I can't. I'm sorry . . . you were called. I didn't mean . . . for you to come. Lo siento." Alberto spoke haltingly, as if every word hurt.

"Carol heard you say the name of some captain. A friend?"

"No, no es amigo." Alberto looked at Grace, hesitated,

and then said, "Please, you should go. Seeing me could be trouble for you."

Grace looked into Alberto's eyes as if in their depths she would find a killer, but all she saw was fear and something tender, fragile. "I know about the lady in the apartment you were painting. A policewoman came to see me."

Alberto lowered his eyes. He covered his ears and then his face. Grace saw his chest shake with sobs. She dreaded what he might say after he stopped crying. How would she respond if he admitted to killing the woman? How could she stay with him if he was a killer? Terror filled her. If he'd killed the woman, Alberto could just as easily kill her. She pulled slightly away from Alberto and glanced at the back door.

Alberto caught his breath and wiped his eyes with his sleeve. "In all my life, I think maybe I cried once when my father died. Now my sister tells me she hears me crying at night and in the past day I've cried three times." Alberto smiled, a forced smile. He went on, "My mind is . . . it gets confused about things like the teapot . . . it cannot control tears when they want to come out . . . it . . . hears a voice that tells me to do things. I call that voice Captain America. I don't do the things it tells me to do. No, I didn't kill the woman. But . . . I'm not sure. Not sure. I want to find out if I did it. If it was me, I will go to the police."

The image of the woman banging her head on the table in the library came to Grace. The fear she had felt then she felt now, but there was something in his voice, a loneliness she recognized. "How? How will you find out?"

"I was going to look for Jimbo. Jimbo Jasmine. He and Lucas were with me painting the woman's house when she was killed. Jimbo may know something that can help me."

"There were others there the day she was killed?"

"My sister told me that Mrs. . . . . Mrs. . . . ."

"Mrs. Macpherson."

"Mrs. Macpherson, she died after Lucas and Jimbo left, when I was there alone."

"Do you know where Jimbo lives?"

"No. In Brownsville someplace." Alberto gasped, grabbed his abdomen. "His mother works in a church near his apartment. I was going to visit the churches in Brownsville today and look for her."

"And then somebody beat you up."

Alberto nodded. Grace felt opposing forces clash

inside her. One part of her wanted to hug him, to comfort him somehow, and another part wanted to bolt out of the pottery studio as fast as humanly possible. Alberto hit the side of his head with his fist a few times. Something inside was even more painful than his mangled ear and crushed cheek. What could she do?

Carol opened the door to the room and entered, out of breath. "Quick, go out the back. A police car just pulled up in front of the store. That woman detective. Hurry. You have to go. Now."

Grace helped Alberto out of the chair. She watched him grab his backpack and then they stepped outside. Grace called a taxi and gave specific instructions where to pick them up.

"Go. Please," Alberto pleaded. "This is no place for you."

"No place for me," she said to herself. Those were the words that explained what she had been feeling for the past couple of months. Why hadn't she thought of them before? When he started to tremble, she put her arm around his shoulder and propped him up.

"Where should we go?" the taxi driver asked when Grace and Alberto were safely in the back seat.

"Drive away from here, for starters," Grace responded.

"You can drop me off in Brownsville. I'll look for Jimbo's mother," Alberto said weakly.

"You can barely walk. We need to find a safe place for you."

They had driven away from Prospect Park and headed down Ocean Avenue toward Coney Island. Where could she take him? Was there a place where she could drop him off gracefully? She chuckled at her own joke. What about her dad? Didn't psychiatrists have a duty to care for the ill? She couldn't see Alberto in her father's dark walnut and soft leather office. Taking him to her apartment was out of the question. Why? She told herself Alberto needed the kind of help neither she nor her mother could give, but she knew that was only partially true. Alberto was an unknown entity, possibly dangerous.

"Ay Dios mío," Alberto groaned, grabbing his head.

The Spanish words reminded Grace of Ernestina. Could Ernestina help? Maybe she knew a place where undocumented immigrants could be treated safely. Maybe. It was a long shot, but Grace was desperate.

Grace tapped the number on her phone. A man's voice answered. Grace didn't know what to say; she was expecting to hear Ernestina's voice. "Joseph?"

"Grace! Is this really you? I was hoping you'd call again. Ernestina went to the store. She forgot her phone and I thought it might be Isabel, her daughter. I'm so glad you called. How are you?"

"Grandfather . . ."

"Please call me Joseph like you've always done."

"Joseph, I was actually calling Ernestina for a favor. A friend, someone I know, was mugged and he's hurt. He can't go to a hospital for a lot of reasons. I think he may be undocumented. I thought maybe Ernestina would know a safe place for him."

"Are you with your friend now?"

"Yes."

"What's his name?"

"Alberto." There was a pause. "I can't think of his last name right now."

"Bring Alberto here to my house. I'll have someone come over and look at him."

"Are you sure?"

"Grace, you don't know me very well, but I don't often say things I don't mean. You know where I live?"

"I have it in my contacts," Grace said, embarrassed.

"Well then, it's time you made use of it. I'll get a bed ready."

Grace found Joseph's address and read it to the cab driver. Alberto shook his head as if trying to object. "I'm not well. Something is broken in me. Not just my body. Inside."

"I know," Grace said, and she thought, *You're not the only one.*

"I forgot to get the bowl you made for me," Alberto whispered.

Grace did not respond to Alberto. Her mind was too full of fear. She was doing something that could easily destroy her bright future, to use Detective Lydell's phrase. What she was doing was not a game. It was serious and real and quite possibly a huge, irreversible mistake.

CHAPTER 14

Joseph and Ernestina were waiting for Grace on the front porch of the house. The porch, the whole one-story, wooden house, looked as if a strong gust of wind would blow it down. The house was painted an ugly egg-yolk color that seemed to make some kind of statement to the rest of Brooklyn. It was squeezed between a five-story apartment building and a busy day care center, so maybe the statement was simply: I was here first and I'm not moving.

Ernestina and Joseph were sitting on two green rocking chairs. Ernestina was texting with one finger on her phone and Joseph was looking straight at Grace getting out of the cab. Grace met his eyes and waved. Then she remembered that Joseph was almost totally blind.

"Grace!" Ernestina shouted. She dropped her phone into the floppy pocket of a flowery apron and then ran to hug Grace. Ernestina was thinner and darker skinned than Grace remembered. Joseph stood and held on to the railing of the porch. Grace and Ernestina helped Alberto out of the car.

"Pero qué te hicieron, muchacho?" Ernestina asked when she saw Alberto's face. She grabbed ahold of Alberto and helped him up the porch steps while Grace paid the taxi driver.

When they reached the top of the porch, Joseph said, "Ernestina, as soon as he's settled, call Rabbi Sacks and tell her that our guest has arrived." Then, to Alberto, in broken Spanish, "Mi casa es tú casa."

"Gracias," Alberto said.

"Necesitas un buen baño," Ernestina said, wrinkling her nose.

When Ernestina and Alberto were inside the house, Joseph reached out, touched Grace's face. "You've grown since the last time I saw you."

What could Grace say? There was no way to explain

why she had never tried to see them. Grace saw Joseph struggling to find the rocking chair and went to him. "Let me help you." Instead of helping Joseph to the chair, she hugged him with all her strength. After a few moments, she started to cry.

"Hey, hey." Joseph pulled away from her and touched Grace's wet cheeks. "What is this? Let's sit and wait here for Rabbi Sacks."

"Who's Rabbi Sacks?" Grace sat in the rocking chair next to Joseph.

Joseph spoke with his head tilted in the direction of Grace. "She's the rabbi of the synagogue that Benny attends. Me too, on occasion. She was a nurse before she became a rabbi. She'll know what to do. Now, tell me what's going on with you."

"I didn't know where to take Alberto. We were so rushed."

"Yes, yes, I want to know more about that, but those tears just now are not about Alberto, are they?"

Grace thought for a few moments. "No, I guess not."

"I didn't think so," Joseph said. The way he said it, Grace thought he knew what was happening to her better than she did. "By the way, your father called Ernestina about a minute before you got here. I'm sorry, I'm afraid

Ernestina told him you were on your way here. I hope he's okay. He was not happy. He's coming over to pick you up as soon as he finishes his business in Manhattan."

"Oh God, the app."

"What?"

"Mom, Dad, and I have a location app in our phones that lets us know where each one is at all times. I forgot to disconnect Dad when he left us."

"An app that lets people know where you are. I'm glad that wasn't around when I was your age."

They both turned when they heard a loud whistling coming from the sidewalk. "That must be Rabbi Sacks. She's always annoyingly chipper."

"I heard that, young man!" Rabbi Sacks did not fit with Grace's picture of a rabbi: a woman in her fifties wearing brown polyester pants a size larger than they needed to be. The dark circles around her very blue eyes contrasted sharply with a silly-looking brown beret that sat loosely on her gray hair. She carried a black doctor's bag in her left hand. Grace stood to shake her hand. "Sit, sit. We don't stand on ceremony here."

"We could use a little ceremony," Joseph quipped.

Rabbi Sacks whacked Joseph on his shoulder. "Shh. I was talking to the young lady. So, you're Grace. A beautiful name. The closest translation in Hebrew would probably be *hesed*. An undeserved kindness and generosity. You must come with Benny to synagogue sometime. Now, where's our patient?"

"He's inside with Ernestina. You might want to moderate your enthusiasm a little when you're with him."

"Oh, shush." When she opened the door, Rabbi Sacks exclaimed, "It always smells so good in here. What is Ernestina cooking this time?"

"Wow," Grace said, after the door had slammed closed again.

"Right? The woman is a force of nature. I'm not sure Rabbi Sacks is exactly what Deborah had in mind when she entrusted me with Benny's religious education, but Benny loves being a Jew and it's because of her."

"I'm sure Benny would not feel that way if he had stayed in our family."

"You know, when Deborah passed away, I did not even believe in God."

"And now?"

"I like what Rabbi Sacks said in one of her sermons. She said that faith happens after you start walking, not before. That's what I'm doing—walking. But it's good to have a direction."

Grace nodded, then paused. "What direction?" she asked.

"Oh, Rabbi Sacks says the direction is toward holiness, but that's above my pay grade. I keep it simple: I study Torah with Benny and I try to do a good deed when there's no avoiding it!" Joseph chuckled. "That's about as holy as I can get."

Grace remembered how she'd felt when Carol called earlier that morning. She resented being asked to help Alberto. "Doing a good deed is not as easy as it sounds."

"Especially when we don't want to." The way Joseph said this, Grace had the impression he had read her thoughts. Joseph patted Grace's arm. "Do you know that your mother calls Ernestina every couple of weeks to check up on me and Benny?"

"No! I had no idea. Why would she not tell me that?"

"Ernestina has a way of getting people to open up. Your mother talks to her about the divorce. Sometimes I eavesdrop. I don't know what goes on in Maury's head. How could he leave you and your mother? I take it personally. This is the boy Leah and I raised? I wish she was still with us. She would set him straight."

The front door opened, and Rabbi Sacks stepped out.

The happy face had been replaced by a worried look. Rabbi Sacks pulled a wooden folding chair from the other end of the porch. She sat next to Joseph, preoccupied.

Joseph spoke first. "This is strange. Ten seconds went by without you saying a word."

"I wish I could send him to Mount Sinai to get some X-rays and an MRI. I don't think anything is broken and probably no internal bleeding, but without tests . . . Anyway, I took care of him as best I could. Some ibuprofen, some rest. I gave him something to help him sleep. Physically he'll be okay."

"Physically?" Grace asked.

"He's scared." Rabbi Sacks said.

Grace knew Rabbi Sacks was waiting for an explanation. How much should she tell Rabbi Sacks, or Joseph, for that matter? Would people stop helping Alberto if they knew he was wanted by the police? Would she get in trouble for helping a criminal? "He's undocumented," Grace said, avoiding Rabbi Sacks's eyes.

"Oh, come on! It's more than that." Rabbi Sacks looked intently at Grace.

Grace gulped, then stammered, "He . . . told me . . . he heard a voice. A voice that tells him to do things. He calls it Captain America."

"Schizophrenia?" Joseph asked.

"We need a mental health professional to determine that," Rabbi Sacks said. "Hearing a voice is not uncommon in the book I spend my life reading. Anyway, putting a name to his condition is not needed right now. What we know for sure is that he needs help."

"Our help," Joseph said.

"Well, he came to us, didn't he?" Rabbi Sacks was quiet for a few seconds and then her face suddenly brightened again. "He's going to sleep for a while. I'll be back in a couple of hours."

Ernestina came out a few moments later. "I'm going to the drugstore to pick up some things. You better go see him before he falls asleep," she said to Grace.

Grace turned to leave, but Joseph held her. "Tell him he can stay as long as he wants."

Alberto was trying to remember how he'd killed Mrs. Macpherson. He had an image of hitting her over the head with something heavy made of silver, but he didn't know whether the image came from what he did or from what Lupe told him. There was something about the lady doctor, a kindness in the way she asked him questions and then waited for his answer that made him tell her about Captain America. Captain America was the hurt that needed the most healing. *How do I shut him up?* he asked the doctor. What was her name? He could not remember. Ernestina called her rabbi. A rabbi was like a priest, no? He could confess to her everything. He killed a defenseless old woman and then stole Wayne's money. He should have grabbed his Captain America comic book while he was at it. But where did he put the money? And the gun. Why did he take the gun? That didn't make sense.

Now here was Grace sitting at the edge of the bed next to him. She was beautiful. He wanted to kiss her. Their kisses would be gentle, as if their lips were the petals of the cherry blossom tree that the wind could take at any moment. Ah, he remembered the name of a tree. He had told Grace about Mrs. Macpherson and about Captain America and she had stayed with him. He felt the surge of tears making its way from his chest to his eyes. No, no, please, no more tears. Why all the crying?

"Are you awake?" Grace asked.

Alberto noticed that his chest was bare. He crossed his arms. "Ernestina says I need a bath very bad."

"I would agree with that," Grace joked.

Alberto pointed with his chin to the bookshelf behind Grace. "The boy that lives here is very smart. Ernestina said he's twelve years old. But look at those books."

Grace glanced at some of the titles. *The Essential Talmud. God in Search of Man. The Lonely Man of Faith.* "Whew!" Then on one of the walls she saw a poster of a boy on a flying dragon.

Alberto followed her gaze and smiled when he saw the poster. "But he's still a little boy," he said.

"What will you do?" Grace asked, her voice almost a whisper.

"I will rest here for an hour. Take a bath and then leave."

"I think my grandfather is okay with you staying."

Alberto shook his head. "No, no. I need to go to Brownsville and find the church where Jimbo's mother works."

"Rabbi Sacks is coming back this afternoon. You should talk to her. About the voice. About whatever you want. Everything you say to her will be confidential."

"I have told you more than I should. You cannot be involved."

Grace held Alberto's hand. "I may already be involved."

She thought she felt his hand pull her gently toward

him. Or maybe she imagined the tender pull and the force that drew her to him was one of those she should have learned more about in her physics class. His eyes closed a second before she kissed him.

Alberto's eyes were still closed when she pulled away from him. He whispered something but she couldn't quite make out what he said. She only heard her name. She liked the way he said it, as if he was afraid of her leaving. "That was kind of unexpected," she said, trying to catch her breath.

Alberto didn't answer. His eyes were closed, and he was breathing with his mouth slightly open, like a child. He was fast asleep.

He hadn't even been aware of their kiss. There was no reason for her to tell Michael about it. Grace touched the purple-and-yellow flesh around his eyes. His wounded face was no longer stunning the way it was when he first entered the apartment, but it was beautiful in a different way. Why did she want to be close to him and run the hell away from him?

She reached out and touched his long hair with the tips of her fingers. How was it that this mentally ill person, this fugitive from the police, had entered her heart?

CHAPTER 15

Grace sat on a rocking chair, watching people walk by the house. Joseph had gone in to avoid an awkward scene with her father. She checked her phone and read a post from Michael: All your hard work paid off, my love—the next valedictorian of BP! Attached was a picture of Grace pointing at the sign: BOLLARD PREPARATORY ACADEMY—WHERE EXCELLENCE IS MADE. Michael's post had received one hundred and forty likes and twenty-six shares. A text arrived from Stella:

Where are you? Are you home sick? You have to
tell me when you're not coming to school. I worry.
Congrats on valedictorian—not that I ever doubted it!

Grace went through her messages. Teachers, friends, people she barely knew were congratulating her. There was even a message from Paul Fleming.

Hey Grace, if it couldn't be me, I'm glad it was you.
Really, a big way to go from me!

Paul and Grace had been competing in a friendly way for the number one spot in the class since their first year in high school. They alternated with Paul taking one semester and Grace the next. If someone slipped, it was because they got an A-minus and the other got a straight A.

Making valedictorian was what Grace had worked for since the first day of high school. During her junior year she had started working on the valedictorian speech. She could, if asked, recite it at that very moment. A week ago, making valedictorian would have made Grace extremely happy. Now she couldn't understand why she had put so much energy and effort into the pursuit.

But why was the announcement made now instead of at the end of the year when all the grades were in? If the decision was made at the end of the school year, she would need an A in physics, and there was no way she would have gotten an A if she'd taken the test last Monday. Not with the few hours of study that she had put in. It seemed unfair that the selection was made more than a month before the end of school. She opened the website to Bollard Preparatory Academy on her phone and found the school's academic policy. There, she read:

The valedictorian is the student with the highest academic average on the date that is forty-five days before the last scheduled day of school. The valedictorian shall give the valedictory address at the commencement ceremony.

Grace subtracted forty-five days from the day she knew to be the last day of school. It was sheer luck that the cutoff date had been last Monday, the day she'd stayed home sick and missed her physics exam. It was her good fortune and Paul's bad. Good luck usually translates into a feeling of happiness, no? Then why did she feel so crappy?

The phone vibrated in her hand. Michael. She didn't answer. She didn't feel like being congratulated or explaining where she was. She sighed. She was in a different world here, sitting in a creaky rocking chair in a house painted egg-yolk yellow. How did making valedictorian compare, merit wise, with an old blind man taking in a stranger who hears voices? Joseph and Ernestina and Rabbi Sacks were like, *of course we'll take care of him.* They didn't even blink.

Reentering was going to be hard. The world she had inhabited the past five hours was complicated, mysterious, scary compared to the simple, straightforward, goal-oriented world she lived in at home and at school. The high-rise life she was returning to was perfect for forgetting about the *direction* that Joseph spoke about. She was going back to a place where everyone was going someplace important, but no one knew why.

She saw her father's black BMW roll slowly down the street. The car stopped in front of the house and she saw the look of disgust in her father's face before he noticed her on the front porch. He waved, a little wiggle of the fingers, and then he opened the passenger door from inside the car. He seemed relieved when he saw Grace come up to the car.

Grace got in the front and threw her backpack in the back seat. She took one last look at the house as her father drove away. "You want to get some lunch?" her father asked.

"Thank you, no."

"Cup of coffee?"

"Thanks, no."

"We should talk, Gracie."

Grace was silent. They were passing by a children's playground. It looked abandoned. Two of three swings were broken and there were beer cans and paper bags all throughout the fenced-in area. "We can talk there."

Her father gave her a look, but found a parking space next to the playground. They both got out at the same time. Grace heard the beep of the car doors locking behind her. Grace glanced at her father as he examined the graffiti on the bench before sitting. Maurice Reuben was fifty-one years old. He was short, wiry, and prematurely bald, but he was fit and elegant in his light gray suit. He was wearing a pink shirt with a white collar and violet-and-blue-striped tie. When they sat, Grace could tell that he was analyzing the connection between the place where she wanted to talk and her psyche. His forehead was wrinkled with concern.

"I'm okay, Dad, really."

Her father crossed his legs gingerly and flicked away a speck of lint from his thigh. He looked up, perhaps to see if it had come from above. Grace had always admired her father's professionalism. He once told her he wore a suit to work every day even though his office was in the basement floor of their brownstone, to inspire confidence in his clients and to show respect for them and their suffering. The same respect that he did not show her mother or her. Maybe her mother was right and at the bottom of the sudden dissatisfaction with Grace's life was anger at her father finally boiling over. There he was now, sitting uncomfortably, waiting for her to let him in.

"What does love mean to you, Dad?" Because life's too important to fool around with little questions.

Her father jerked back instinctively. "Wow," he said finally. "You don't mess around."

"I know it sounds like I'm blaming you for divorcing us, Mom and me . . . maybe I am." Grace took a deep breath. Anger began to simmer. She made a mental note to be . . . to be what? The only word she could think about was *professional*. She took another deep breath and continued, "Right now I'm asking for personal reasons. I want to know what love is. Is it a feeling that goes away? Is it an obligation that keeps people bound to each other even when they don't feel like it? Is it a decision that a person makes?"

"You're angry at me, I understand."

"No, you don't understand. Yes, I am angry." The hell with being professional. "I need to understand what was going through your mind. You told Mom that you weren't growing together anymore and that the marriage was, quote-unquote, 'thwarting' your individual growth. You told her that you loved her but were no longer 'in love' with her. What the hell does that mean? Don't you see how Mom and I don't understand? Don't you see how that affects me? How a divorce from Mom is a divorce from me? You even took away our home, the place where I grew up."

It might have been the first time that Grace saw her father's face turn a brilliant red. He was either angry or ashamed or both. "I had to fight for that house. It's my livelihood. I was entitled to much more under the laws of New York. I gave up on all the rest, but the basement floor of the house is where my clients have come to find solace. I couldn't take that away from them."

"I don't want to fight, Dad, honestly. Most of all I want to understand how love works. When should two people come together? When should they fight to stay together?" Grace thought of Alberto. Someone she had met only twice. Was what she felt touching his lips, his bruised face, a love that would last forever? And if it was, how would they exist together? She'd go with him to Mexico, get a job making pottery? "It's all so confusing," Grace said, forgetting for a moment that her father was sitting next to her.

"I'm not sure I understand how love works," her father said. "Does anybody? There would be lots less books and lots less beautiful music if we understood."

"And lots less psychiatrists."

"And lots less psychiatrists." Her father started to laugh but turned serious when he saw the tears roll down Grace's cheek. He drew closer and was about to put his arm around her, but she shook her head to let him know that she did not want to be touched. "Oh, Gracie, I'm so sorry, honey."

"I don't even know why I'm crying," Grace said, wiping her tears with the back of her hand.

"Your mother thinks I'm responsible for what you're going through."

"It's not always about you, Dad." Grace immediately regretted the bitter tone.

"Okay, maybe not always, but what about this time? How long have you been feeling sad?"

"Dad, stop it. I'm not one of your patients. This is not the onset of a clinical depression."

"No? How many times have you cried in the past week?"

She cried when she saw Joseph. She cried with Michael. She cried with her mother. Maybe another time or two. Okay, so that was unusual for her. But did that mean there were no reasons for the tears? The tears felt appropriate when they came. Like they were long overdue. What could she say? Sadness came with a question, asking her where she was going. That was as close to the truth as she could figure out, but how could she possibly explain what she didn't fully understand? Grace decided to change the subject. She wiped her eyes with her hand and cleared her throat. "Can I ask you a question?" Grace did not wait for a reply. "What would you do if someone came to you and said he heard a voice? A voice that asked him to do things?"

"I would assess if he was a danger to himself or others.

I would send him to one of my neurologist colleagues to rule out any brain pathologies. I would—"

"But how would you determine if he was a danger to himself or others?"

"His words, his actions, his history, his body language. That kind of determination is both a science and an art. I would listen to him with my whole self, heart and mind."

"And if the voice asked him to hurt others?"

"I would take that into account, but that wouldn't be the only determinative in my assessment. The large, large majority of persons with schizophrenia, one of the mental illnesses where auditory hallucinations may be found, are not violent. They may hear a command for violence but will not act it out. Similar to when you or I are on top of a skyscraper and the thought of jumping comes to us."

Grace was silent, thinking. Listening to her father reminded her of why she had wanted to be a psychiatrist since she was ten years old. It wasn't so much that she wanted to be a psychiatrist as that she wanted to be like him: the person who listened to her as if every word was a miracle not to be missed.

"Dad? Can I ask you one more question?"

"I think you will do it no matter what I say."

"Why were you so opposed to Benny going to live with Joseph?"

Grace saw her father swallow, look away from her. She stared at him and waited. When he finally spoke, his words were tinged with anger. "Religion is at best an escape and a fraud, at worst an evil. I didn't want Benny to be a part of that. Benny would have been better off with us. He'd be strong and independent and self-sufficient, like you."

Grace laughed softly. "Funny, I don't feel all those wonderful things." Before her father could respond, Grace stood. "Can you take me home? There's something I need to do."

On the way back to the car, her father said, "If you needed a quiet place to get away, you can always stay with me. Your room is always there, waiting for you."

"Thank you," she said, entering the car.

"You know I love you, don't you?" Her father rested his hand on her shoulder when she was seated. She nodded like someone who knew the words would be coming. "And please let me know how I can help—with the questions you have about schizophrenia."

Maybe he's not a total jerk, Grace said to herself.

She took her laptop out of her backpack as soon as she entered her apartment. During the ride home with her father she kept thinking about what Rabbi Sacks had said: *What we know for sure is that he needs help.* That's what she wanted to do. Help Alberto find out if he was innocent by locating Jimbo, which meant finding the church where Jimbo's mother worked. Grace wasn't sure how Jimbo could help Alberto since, according to Alberto, they were already gone when Mrs. Macpherson was killed. But Alberto thought it was good place to start and she wanted to honor that.

In her room, sitting at her desk, she found twenty-one churches in Brownsville. She wrote down their phone numbers and started calling them on her cell phone. When someone answered, she asked if she could talk to Mrs. Jasmine. On the twentieth call, a man who sounded as if he had no teeth, said, "No asmin, asmeen."

"Mrs. Jasmeen? Is she there?" Grace asked, her heartbeat quickening.

"Ee only comes on aturdays now. Ey cut er hours."

"On Saturdays?"

"Es!"

"Do you have her address, by any chance? I was thinking of hiring her."

"Old on."

Please. Please. Have her address, Grace said to herself. She laughed at the thought that she quite possibly had just prayed.

"No aress. Come ere on aturday. See er. Ate o welve."
Click.

Grace wrote down the name and address of the church, then went on Google Maps. Our Lady of the Presentation was a forty-five-minute walk from Joseph's house. Grace was almost certain that the old man's last words were eight to twelve. She tapped Joseph's number.

"It's me," she said when Ernestina answered. "How's Alberto?"

"He's still sleeping. And as soon as he wakes up, he's going to take a much-needed bath."

Grace giggled. "Do you have pen and paper? I have an address for Alberto."

"Yep, right here."

Grace gave Ernestina the name of the church and the address. "Tell him Mrs. Jasmine is only there on Saturday from eight to twelve." She thought for a moment and then said, "Tell him I'll be there around eight."

"Okay. I'll tell him. And Grace?"

"Yes?"

"You did good today."

Grace stared at her phone after Ernestina hung up. She had done good? Then why did she feel as if she had just unloaded a problem into someone else's lap?

I did what I could. I took him to a safe place. I found the church where his friend's mother works. That's enough, isn't it? What more can I do? I can't help him anymore. I shouldn't have told Ernestina that I'll be at the church. Why did I do that?

And the kiss? And the tenderness and hunger I feel?

Grace had no answers to her own questions.

CHAPTER 16

Alberto and Benny sat on the floor of Benny's room. Benny's laptop was between them. Benny was showing Alberto pictures of his mother. Alberto was anxious. He wanted to leave as soon as possible, but Ernestina was washing his clothes and all he was wearing was Joseph's pajamas. He was also enjoying Benny's company. The boy reminded him of Chela, his little sister in Ticul. They were kids, but they were smarter than him in many ways.

When they finished, Benny began playing a strange but beautiful melody on his harmonica. It sounded like the kind of music you would hear in church, only you could almost dance to it. Alberto closed his eyes and began rocking back and forth just like Benny was doing. Some of the music had a happy, fast tempo and some of it was sad, with a melody that made Alberto wish he could be with his mother and sisters at that very moment. But the best part was that the music swept away the presence of Captain America.

As soon as Benny finished playing, Alberto heard voices coming from the living room. Joseph was talking to someone. "It's Papa talking on the phone to Rabbi Sacks." Benny went out of the room. It seemed like a long time went by before Benny returned. When he came in, Alberto closed the laptop.

Benny sat down and asked, "Do you think it's okay to hate people that are very bad?"

"I don't know." Alberto tried to think of people he hated. Did he hate Captain America? "Why do you ask that?"

"Ernestina told me that Camilo, the owner of the bodega down the street, got robbed today. He got hit on the face like you. Camilo is always good to me. I hate the people that hit him even if I don't know them. Do you hate the people that beat you?"

"No, I don't hate them. What good would it do me to hate them?"

"What if you see them again and you have to fight them? Do you need to hate someone to fight them?"

"No, I don't think so. Maybe a little hate. Just enough to fight good."

"Have you fought many people?"

"I never fought anyone."

Benny was quiet, thinking. He wiped his harmonica on his pants. Then he said, "Did Captain America beat you up?"

"How do you know about Captain America?"

"You were still sleeping when I came home from school. I could hear you shouting, 'Leave me alone, Captain America.'"

Alberto nodded. "I'm scared of Captain America . . . sometimes."

"I know why you're scared."

"What?"

"It has to do with thoughts in your head. Maybe you can't control the thoughts that appear in your head. It happens to me too. That's why music helps you, like it helps me."

"Is that what happens to you?"

"Some of the thoughts that appear in here are very bad." Benny tapped his forehead. "I want to kill the bullies that hit Camilo."

"But it is different for me. It's not thoughts." Alberto stopped. "I *hear* words. Like someone outside of me, only the voice is inside. It's hard to describe. Not just any words but a voice that says things about me, that sees what I do, that calls me names, that tells me to do things."

Alberto looked at Benny's face for signs of fear or shock, but there were none. Benny looked as if he was trying to remember something. Why did it feel so right to talk to this boy? Benny was a boy, and Alberto was a man, and yet it felt as if the boy was an equal, a friend he could trust.

Finally, after a long while, Benny said, "Lots of people in the Tanakh, our scriptures, hear the Holy One speak to them."

"The voice I hear is not a holy voice," Alberto said. "It's mean and ugly."

Benny's eyes filled with tears. "It must hurt so much."

"Yes," Alberto said. It was true. He had never thought about it, but it hurt. Every time Captain America spoke, it hurt. The voice was a nail hammered into his head. It was also painful not being able to stop Captain America from speaking. "I don't know why I told you. Maybe because I must leave, and I want you to know why. It's not because I'm not grateful. I like it here with you and your grandfather and Ernestina."

"Why must you leave?"

"I'm afraid. What if Captain America is more powerful than me? What if I'm not strong enough to fight him when he shouts and shouts at me to do something bad?"

"Will you do something bad when he tells you?"

"No. I don't know. I may have already."

May have? You killed the old woman!

"I'm not afraid of Captain America," Benny said after a few moments of reflection. "You shouldn't be either."

The pottery piece that Alberto most loved to make in Ticul was a small rose-colored bowl painted with fierce Maya warriors armed and ready for battle. That's the image that came to Alberto as he watched Benny walk out of the room.

Grace and Michael sat across from Stella and Miriam on the small table that separated the kitchen from the living room. The table was full of paper plates and plastic containers of Chinese food. Michael had brought a bottle of champagne and Miriam had taken out her pink crystal flutes to toast the new valedictorian. No one mentioned Grace's absence from school that day. Grace was grateful her mom had not said anything about the meeting with her dad at the playground even though she was sure her dad had called her. The conversation was animated, bubbly, like the champagne. Grace thought she was doing a good job of blending in with the celebratory mood, but now and then she would catch her mother looking at her with concerned eyes.

"So, let's get a preview of the speech." Michael poured champagne into her glass.

"Michael," Stella said, "give the girl a break, she just found out!"

"Oh, please," Michael responded, "she's been working on it for years. Hey, my dad can give you some good Confucius quotes."

Grace remembered the speech. There was a lot of stuff about dreams and about grit. The grit to make our dreams come true. The speech seemed to have been written by someone else. If she gave that speech now, she'd be an actor performing on the stage. "I could use a little wisdom right now." Grace tried to smile.

"Here's one he gave me that I'm still trying to figure out. Ready?"

"Oh boy." Stella made a funny face and Grace finally smiled.

"No, please, I'm serious. I don't get this one," Michael continued. "It goes like this: 'Don't give a sword to a man who can't dance.' I mean, can someone please tell me what that even means?"

"Maybe your dad wants you to think about that for a while," Miriam said. Then to Grace, "Do you have any idea what you will say?"

"I thought I did," Grace said softly. Then, turning to Michael, "I like that quote, though."

"You know what it means? Please tell me."

"I don't know," Grace said. "Something about dancing and fighting. Both are connected, needed."

The room was suddenly silent. Grace told herself to not be such a downer. These were the people she loved and they were here for her.

"I tell you one thing," Stella said, breaking the silence. "I'm glad I won't have to listen to Paul Fleming for fifteen minutes. He's such a nice guy but soooo . . ."

"Boring!" Michael completed Stella's sentence.

"All right." Rabbi Sacks placed the stethoscope inside her black bag. "I think you're going to live." She pulled out a chair and sat. Alberto put on one of Joseph's T-shirts. "Now what is this about you wanting to leave tonight?"

"It's better if I do."

"Why? You ready to go home?"

Don't talk to this bitch!

"I can't go home."

"Because of the voice you hear," Rabbi Sacks asked quietly.

Alberto looked at her. It wasn't just Captain America. It was also what he might have done to Mrs. Macpherson. Could he tell all of that to this woman? How many people was he willing to drag into the mud pit of his problems? "It tells me bad things. I'm afraid." That was all that the kind woman needed to know.

Strike her in the head like you did the old woman.

"You're afraid you might hurt Joseph or Benny or Ernestina."

"Yes."

"And do you? Want to hurt them?"

"No! Me, Alberto, whoever I am, doesn't want to."

"But this voice tells you to do things? And do you obey it?"

"No. I always fight him. But what if I, whoever I am,

disappears and he makes me do things, moves my body like a puppet, and later I don't remember?"

You remember. Don't pretend you don't.

Rabbi Sacks let out a long sigh. Alberto remembered his mother's face when he said goodbye to her at the bus station in Ticul. "I am no expert, but it looks to me like you, Alberto, are in charge and will continue to be in charge. Oh, how I wish you'd let me take you to a good doctor friend I have at Mount Sinai."

"It's not possible."

"Okay, not now, I understand. But there is help for what you are going through. Please remember that. This is by no means a hopeless situation. Tons of people live happy, fulfilled lives with conditions similar to what you are experiencing."

Rabbi Sacks waited for a response and when she saw Alberto's blank face, said, "Well, here's what I think we should do for the time being. I understand why you don't want to stay with Joseph and Benny because of what you might do. There's a room in the basement of our synagogue, our church, where you can sleep tonight. You'll be all alone and cannot hurt anyone. Okay? I have some ideas where you may stay after that. Safe places. But let's deal with that tomorrow. What do you think?"

Hell no! You'll regret it! I'll make sure!

Alberto nodded. Then he said, "Tomorrow I will find a place."

"Okay." Rabbi Sacks stood. "Let's take it one day at a time. I'll go get the room ready. Ernestina has made you some of her delicious lentil soup. After you eat, she'll bring you over to the synagogue. I'll go inform Joseph."

"I don't want Joseph and Benny to think I'm not grateful."

Rabbi Sacks sat down again, leaned toward Alberto. "Joseph and Benny already know you are grateful, but it wouldn't matter to them if you weren't. They will understand why you don't want to stay here."

"Benny will understand?"

"Yes. Not because he believes you might hurt him, but because he really likes you and cares about you. You made a friend, and let me tell you, that is no small thing. The truth is that you cannot fight this Captain America alone. You're afraid to drag us into the messed-up world of your mind, but no one here's afraid of getting messy. Living in the mess and struggling with the mess is what we are asked to do. The only reason you're spending the night alone is because it will make you feel better. Do you understand what I'm saying to you, son?"

"Yes."

"What am I saying to you?"

"I am not alone."

Grace had just turned off the lamp next to her bed when Miriam entered the room, sat on the edge of the bed, and stroked Grace's hair.

"I'm sorry I ruined the celebration," Grace said. She could not contain the sadness in her voice.

"Oh, sweetie. You didn't ruin anything. You've had quite a day."

"Dad called you after he and I talked?"

"He did."

"It was so good to see Joseph and Ernestina. Benny was at school. I want to see Joseph and Benny frequently. I want to spend time with them. I don't care what Dad says."

"I think that could be arranged. I mean, what's your dad going to do, divorce us?"

When they stopped laughing, Grace said, "Mom, do you think something's wrong with me for not getting excited about being valedictorian?"

"No, I wouldn't say it's 'wrong.' But . . . it could be a sign of something. Maybe your father's right about possible depression. He gave me the name of a colleague who specializes in adolescent . . . issues. Her office is within walking distance."

Grace stared at the ceiling. She missed the luminescent stars on the ceiling of her old bedroom. When she couldn't sleep, she drew imaginary lines from star to star until she could make out the image of a lion. Now the ceiling above her was a big white space and when the lights went out, it would be a big black space, and she wished she had something up there she could try to make into a pattern.

"All of the doubts, the questions, the sadness, are just a chemical imbalance," Grace said quietly to herself.

"It's normal to lose steam at this point when you've been going at it so hard for so long."

"I *am* pretty steam-less right now, Mom. Talk tomorrow?" Grace grabbed her mother's hand and put it on her cheek.

"Okay, honey." Miriam leaned on the bed and hugged Grace. "Just so you know, I'm all for you finding your own path, but that doesn't mean you have to do it on your own. We all could use a little help figuring out what is us and not us. You don't have to be depressed to talk to someone who can help you sort things out. I'll leave you the name and phone of the therapist just in case. In the meantime, take it easy, one step at a time. Keep sharing with me. I'm so grateful that you do."

The room went totally dark when Miriam closed the bedroom's door. There was a faint murmur of cars in the street ten floors below. Grace jumped out of bed and looked for her backpack. Inside she found her physics book. She sat at her desk, tried to brush the image of Alberto away, and began reading.

After supper, they moved to the living room for the nightly Torah study. Alberto sat next to Benny on the sofa and listened to the story that Benny read. This was not one of the stories he had heard from Father Solis during his preparation for First Communion. But this was a good story. He liked the way Abraham haggled with God about the number of good people that Abraham had to find, or else God would destroy Sodom and Gomorrah. God started with fifty and Abraham got him down to ten.

"What do you think?" Joseph asked Alberto.

"Abraham is smart," Alberto said.

"I like the arguments he uses to convince the Holy One," Benny said, clapping his hands. Then, lowering his voice to sound like Abraham: "'Wilt thou indeed destroy the righteous with the wicked? Far be it from you to do such a thing.'"

"Abraham sounds like my mother when she goes to the mercado." Alberto imitated a woman's voice. "'I come to you for ten years because you're the only honest butcher in Ticul and all you give me is fat and bone.'"

They all laughed, and then Joseph said, "I asked Benny to read that passage tonight because I wanted you to hear it."

"Me?" Alberto touched his chest.

"Yes, because if Abraham can stand up to the Creator, you can stand up to a voice that has no meat, no power, no guts."

"Papa!" Benny exclaimed. "You're a rebbe!"

Joseph started to speak when there was a loud knock on the door. Benny jumped up and looked out the front window. "It's a woman, Papa. I don't know her."

Joseph shouted from his chair. "Who is it?"

"NYPD! Open the door!"

"They're coming for me," Alberto said. "I'll go with them."

"Why?" Joseph asked, shocked. "What did you do?"

"A woman was killed . . ." Alberto stammered. "In the apartment I painted. The police say it was me."

"Did you? Did you kill her?" Joseph ignored the persistent knocking.

Alberto closed his eyes. He told himself to tell what he knew. "No. I don't think so. I don't know. I'm trying to find out if I did, if Captain America made me do it."

"Benny." Joseph stretched his hand and waited for Benny to take it. "Go out the back door and take Alberto to Rabbi Sacks."

"Yes, Papa."

"Help me up," he whispered to Benny. Then he shouted: "Coming! I'm blind. It will take me a minute."

"You'll get in trouble," Alberto said to Joseph, resisting the pull of Benny's arm.

"Go, now!" Joseph ordered.

"Please, Alberto," Benny pleaded.

Listen to the kid! I got plans for you.

Alberto ran to Benny's room for his backpack with the broken picture of his family and then followed Benny out the back door of the house.

CHAPTER 17

The small room in the basement of Temple Israel was filled with children's books. Rabbi Sacks prepared for him a cot with green sheets and an orange-and-red bedspread. She brought a cassette recorder and showed him how to use it. The music from the tapes was like the songs that Benny played on his harmonica.

"I just talked to Joseph," Rabbi Sacks said, pulling out a chair from a desk and sitting. "Benny is safely back home. A woman detective was asking about you. She searched the house but didn't find anything about you. That was a close one."

Your girlfriend called the police.

"No, that's not true."

"Pardon me?"

Alberto sat on the edge of the cot. "When the police-woman knocked on the door, Joseph told Benny to bring me here. He acted so quick."

"That's Joseph."

"Why? Why did he not even hesitate to turn me over to the police? Why is he helping me? And now you. Why take such a risk? I may be guilty."

No maybes about it.

Rabbi Sacks let out a long sigh. She looked up at the window near the ceiling for a long time. Finally, she said, "If you did something wrong, we are not going to protect you from the consequences of your action. Did you kill the woman?"

"I'm not sure."

Liar!

"I think Joseph wanted to keep you away from the police to give you a chance to prove that you didn't do it. Our legal system can be unfair to poor people. But . . ." Rabbi Sacks waited for Alberto to meet her eyes. "You should have told Joseph and me you were wanted by the police."

"I'm sorry." Alberto grabbed his head. "My head . . . it's not good."

"I may be wrong, who knows, but I think this is good." Rabbi Sacks pointed at Alberto's heart. "Now it's time to rest. Tomorrow is another day." Just before leaving, Rabbi Sacks pointed to the small window near the ceiling of the room. "I leave the lights on outside to keep kids from coming in at night and partying back there. If you hear noises outside, it's probably them. Just let them be. I've called the police so many times they don't listen to me anymore. I can put a pillow on the window to block the light."

Alberto looked at Rabbi Sacks's face and realized that she had been speaking to him and he had not understood a word. Something about the police. "Thank you" was all he could think of saying. "I will be okay."

Alberto lay on the cot, thinking. There was something he wanted to do tomorrow. What was it? How was he going to send money to his mother? He touched his lips. He had a dream that Grace had kissed him. The kiss felt like the pink petals of that tree in the park. Grace knew the name of the tree and told him. What was it? Lucas said that Wayne had a wife someplace. What was the name of the woman who died?

You mean the one you killed.

In the dream Grace kissed him even after he told her about Mrs. Macpherson. There, her name came back to him. The one good thing he did today was he didn't lie. He told Grace and Joseph and Benny, Ernestina, Rabbi Sacks, he told them about Captain America.

You did lie. Did you tell them the police were after you?

Captain America was right. He had lied by not telling them the full truth, and because of that Joseph might be in trouble. One thing was certain, he could no longer be around them. He couldn't. The police were after him. Where could he go?

Get your ass back to Mexico!

"I need to work so I can help Mamá."

Get Wayne's money. Take it with you.

"I don't know where it is."

You're a miserable liar. Check the loose board in your closet.

Alberto jumped out of the cot. He couldn't breathe. He needed air. He got dressed and found a door that led outside. He sat on the steps that led to a parking lot in the back. He remembered the loose floorboard in the closet of his room. He lifted the board one day and thought it would be a good hiding place for valuables.

He had never used it. But what if he had hidden Wayne's money there? He did not remember doing it, but apparently Captain America did. Who was Captain America anyway? Captain America was him, a part of him. He wasn't some devil that entered his head. When Captain America cussed at him, it was him cussing at himself. Captain America didn't kill Mrs. Macpherson. He did.

"Me. Alberto Bocel. I did it. Yo soy Captain America."

You wish! You're nothing but excrement.

Alberto heard laughter. At first, he thought it was Captain America. Then Alberto heard someone speak in a language he had never heard before. He climbed up the stairs and saw two men sitting at the edge of the parking lot. A third one had a can of spray paint in his hand and was writing a word with big red letters on the back wall of the synagogue. They were about his age, maybe a little older. One of them, the one with the spray can, was as tall as Alberto, but thinner. The other two were short and stocky. One of the short men, the one with a shaved head, had a bottle of liquor on his hand. They stopped laughing when they saw him.

"Who the hell are you?" The man with the shaved head stood and waved the bottle in front of Alberto's face.

"You shouldn't do that," Alberto said, pointing at the wall.

The tall one dropped the can and walked up to Alberto. "Are you the janitor or something?"

These are my kind of people!

Alberto squinted, tried to decipher the giant red letters. He could make out something that looked like an *A.* "Why do you do that? This church doesn't belong to you."

"Does it belong to you?" The tall man took a step closer to Alberto.

"No," Alberto answered calmly. "It belongs to a friend." It felt good to call Rabbi Sacks a friend. She had offered him a safe place to stay even after she found out he was wanted by the police. She protected him and now he could protect what was dear to her.

"Yeah?" The tall man turned to admire his work. "I think the wall looks better now that it has my mark."

"Like an animal," Alberto said, still looking at the wall.

"What you say?" The tall man raised his voice for the first time.

"Animals mark property. But that's not your property to mark." Alberto and the tall man were now inches apart.

"Let's carve him." The man with the shaved head put the bottle on the ground and took out a knife.

Get on your knees! Beg for your life!

Alberto stepped away from the tall man and faced the man with the knife. He walked up to the point of the knife and leaned into it.

Yeah. End it now!

It would be so easy to end it now. Captain America would finally shut up. Alberto would no longer be a danger and a burden for others. A drop of blood stained his shirt. The shiny top of the man's head came up to Alberto's chest. He was looking at Alberto with fear in his eyes. He had not expected a threat to become a real possibility.

Step into the knife! Do it! Now's your chance.

"No!" Alberto shouted, and in one quick movement Alberto lifted the man by the armpits and tossed him on the grass.

No, no. What are you doing?

Alberto held his bruised rib and watched the bald man search for the knife in the grass. When he found it, he said something in that strange language and started after Alberto.

"That's enough," the tall man said, stepping between Alberto and the man with the knife. "How you doing, Shorty?" the tall man asked without taking his eyes from Alberto.

"Son of a bitch caught me by surprise. Let me at him, Dennis."

"You live here?" Dennis asked Alberto.

Ask him to put an end to you.

"Just for the night." Alberto walked to the same spot where the men had been sitting and lowered himself on the grass.

Dennis sat beside him. "Why should you care, then?"

"Rabbi Sacks helped me."

Dennis took out a cigarette and lit it. "You in trouble or something?"

"What's the language you were speaking?" Alberto asked.

"Hey, Dennis. What are we doing here? Let me have a go at him," Shorty said. He had recovered his bottle and was drinking again.

"Albanian. We speak Albanian now and then. That knife didn't scare you, did it?"

Alberto shrugged.

Dennis extended a hand. "I'm Dennis, what's your name?"

"Alberto."

"Alberto. Mmm. Puerto Rican?"

"Mexico."

"Hey, Alberto from Mexico, you're pretty strong, you know that? Shorty weighs about two hundred pounds and you lifted him and tossed him five feet like he was a bag of potatoes. You lift weights?"

"I had a job moving furniture. Now I paint."

Hit him so he can hit you back.

"You look pretty beat-up. Were you in a fight? You want something to drink? Hey, Matt, what are you doing over there? Go get me one of those beers."

Matt was inspecting a pipe next to the back wall of the synagogue. "This is the underground electric cable for the whole place."

"So?" Dennis asked, annoyed.

"We can come back some day and cut off the power when they're all in church."

"You don't have to worry about that right now. Get this man a beer."

"I don't drink," Alberto said. He kept his eyes on

Matt who was jiggling the pipe with the electric cable. The image of his father falling to the ground came to Alberto. He shut his eyes and when he opened them, he asked Dennis: "Are you guys from the CFE?"

"What? CFE? What are you talking about?"

"The electric company."

"Ahh, nooo." Dennis turned toward Shorty. He opened his mouth, raised his eyebrows, and tapped his temple. Shorty laughed. Then Dennis said to Alberto: "Listen, I didn't finish writing my mark. I gotta finish. It looks sloppy, you know."

Alberto shook his head. "I can't let you do that."

Dennis scratched his head, thinking. "Tell you what. If you're not too hurt, there's these fights in a warehouse over in Coney Island. They have them every other week. One's coming up this Saturday. You'd make a good fighter. It's good money. Depending on the crowd. I came out of there with two thousand a couple of weeks ago. Why don't you come? I'll fight you. Look at me, all skin and bones. You come and fight and I'll stop right now. Pick up my cans and go home."

Shorty and Matt laughed.

Say yes. Say yes. Best offer you'll ever get.

"If I go fight, you promise you don't come back to this

church ever again. You promise never to cut the electric power off." Alberto looked deep into Dennis's eyes.

"Deal."

"Coney Island?"

"Look for the handball courts. A block from there will be a door with a green light. You can't miss it."

"I'll forget. My mind's not working . . . good."

I'll get you there.

"Matt, you still got that pencil? Write the directions on a piece of that paper bag."

Matt tore a piece off a brown bag and wrote using Shorty's back for support. He gave the paper to Alberto, who stuck it in his pocket.

"All right," Dennis said. "We'll go now. Just to show you I'm a man of my word."

Dennis whispered in Alberto's face as he was leaving: "Alberto from Mexico versus Dennis the Menace. Sounds good, don't it? That'll get some bets going. Oh, I forgot to tell you. I've never lost."

"You're a piece of dead meat," Shorty shouted.

Alberto thought of going back inside, but all he could do was stretch out on the grassy knoll and lie down. Before falling asleep, he heard Captain America.

Saturday night. A good night to die.

CHAPTER 18

*G*race had stayed up till four a.m. studying physics. Sometime after midnight, when she couldn't sleep, she decided to take the test that Friday rather than wait until Monday. It was either memorizing the equations that describe the motion of an object at constant acceleration or thinking about Alberto and accelerating out of her normal orbit. At six the alarm on her cell phone went off. She showered and got dressed. She heard her mother's alarm clock just as she was leaving the apartment. She did not take the piece of paper with the psychiatrist's phone number that her mother had left for her. She had no intention of seeing a psychiatrist, at least not yet, but she did plan to use the day to assure her mother, Michael, and Stella that she was, more or less, the same old Grace.

Mr. Lerner was sitting at his desk with the same gigantic cup of coffee he'd had since he started teaching twenty or so years ago. Kids called it the Lerner Bowl. It looked like a grapefruit cut in half and carved out. It didn't even have a handle. Mr. Lerner was lifting it to his lips with both hands when he saw Grace at the doorway. He quickly put it down and said, "Grace, you're here early."

"I thought maybe I could take that exam I missed last Monday."

"Now? Are you sure? I have you scheduled to take it on Monday."

Grace answered quickly. "No, I think it'd be better if this test is behind me."

"And, oh, congratulations on making valedictorian. Well deserved."

"I'm not sure it's well deserved. If the grade for this test was taken into account . . ."

"One test score doesn't negate four years of effort," Mr. Lerner said. "Well, okay. If you feel ready. Remember that this exam will count for forty percent of your grade. Right now, you have an A average, so . . ."

Grace could not imagine how she had managed to score so high on the two previous exams. She could not remember what had motivated her to study so hard and so long. She couldn't come up with any reason for the grueling work other than at some point competing to be the best became a compulsion she could not turn off.

"Grace, are you okay?" Mr. Lerner looked concerned. "You're pale."

"Let's do it!"

"Well, okay. Now, you can use your graphing calculator, as you know. Raise your hand when you're ready to start and I'll set my timer for fifty minutes. Good luck."

Grace raised her hand and began to read. The test was five pages long. The first part consisted of ten multiple-choice questions worth three points each. The rest of the exam consisted of ten questions that required explanations and a section of five problems. On top of the page with the problems, Mr. Lerner had typed in bold, capital letters: SHOW YOUR WORK.

Grace saw Mr. Lerner leave the room with the Lerner Bowl in hand. What was Alberto doing now? He was awake by now for sure. He didn't strike her as the kind of person who liked to sleep late. Did he think about her? Grace shook her head and tried to focus. *An object is placed in an elevator descending . . .* Alberto was in that elevator going nowhere. She had hopped on momentarily, but now it was time to get off.

Grace was amazed that she knew as much as she did. She totally punted on three of the problems and on three of the questions requiring an explanation. Assuming she had answered everything else correctly, her score would be seventy-two points out of a possible one hundred. Seventy-two was a C. Her first C in an exam ever. It was a new feeling for her—this being okay with a C. She felt a lot calmer than when she fretted about getting an A-minus instead of an A. She had never known how liberating it was not to care about the outcome of some effort. She had given it her best, all things considered, and that was good enough. The image of Alberto making calaveras came to her mind.

When Mr. Lerner returned, Grace handed him the blue book with her answers. Mr. Lerner flipped through the pages. Now and then he would look up at Grace with an expression of mild shock. Grace was putting her pencil and calculator in her backpack when Mr. Lerner said, "Grace, uh, are you feeling all right? If you're not well, I can tear this up and you can retake it on Monday."

"I feel fine. Thank you."

Grace walked slowly out of the room.

Alberto woke up in the basement room that Rabbi Sacks had prepared for him. He did not remember coming in from outside. For a moment he thought the encounter with the three men had been a dream, but when he looked for his shoes, he couldn't find them. He must have left them outside. There was a piece of paper in his pocket with a date and address. He had no idea what it was or where it came from. He stuffed it inside his backpack. What was happening to him? Forgetting was worse than hearing Captain America. Maybe there was a switch in his brain that Captain America turned off when he wanted to take over.

Alberto found his shoes outside where he had first fallen asleep. He tied his shoes and began to walk at a fast pace. He was suddenly overcome with shame. He had enjoyed picking up and tossing the bald man on the grass. That wasn't Captain America's enjoying, that was him. Did he also take pleasure in killing Mrs. Macpherson?

You liked the knife against your chest.

Alberto had almost obeyed Captain America. Stepping into that knife was tempting. Put an end to Captain America.

Next time listen to me.

Alberto didn't know exactly how, but it was Grace who stopped him from pushing himself against the knife. He felt for her what he had never felt before. It was a yearning more powerful even than his wish to go back home. It was like being lost on a dark night and seeing the light from a window in the distance.

Had he ever been in love? Did he even know what love was? He had been with other girls, like Pilar, who they'd lived with soon after they moved to New York. He'd been asleep on the sofa and woke up to her drunken kisses. Pilar was older than him, older even than Lupe, and she was experienced. What happened that night was not love, although Pilar said it was. That night was two people using each other. Now he felt a powerful desire to be with Grace, so what was the difference between this want and that hunger?

Alberto wished he was smarter, he wished he knew more words, in Spanish or English; he didn't care so long as they could describe what he was feeling. If only he could think and talk like Captain America.

Don't make me laugh.

He had to be strong and resist the urge to be close to Grace or to have her come close to him. If what he felt for her was love, then keeping her away from him was how he could best love her. Grace had a life, a beautiful apartment, a caring mother, a boyfriend. She studied physics. Physics! He had seen the section on physics in his high school equivalency books. Physics was the study of forces and there were four fundamental forces in the universe. Alberto was intimately acquainted with the power of one of them: The electrical component of the electromagnetic force zapped the life out of his father in a fraction of a second. *Zap.* It had taken Alberto one hour to read the introduction to the physics section, an introduction that was only half a page. The thought of him and Grace as an "us" or a "we" was more than ridiculous; it was impossible.

The best thing you can do is zap yourself.

What he needed to do most of all was find out once and for all if he had killed Mrs. Macpherson. Ernestina had given him Grace's message with the address for Mrs. Jasmine, but she wouldn't be at work until tomorrow, Saturday. Today he decided to go to Lupe's apartment. Lupe could give him more information about the murder and what the police knew. He would also check under the loose floorboard in his room. If he found Mrs. Macpherson's things and Wayne's money and gun, there would be no doubt.

You killed her.

Alberto was practically running. It was funny that he always called it Lupe's apartment even though he lived there as well. When Lupe was seven months pregnant, Wayne made a big deal of giving Lupe the keys to the apartment. He gave Lupe a set of keys tied to a tiny diamond ring. Lupe called it an engagement ring even though she knew that Wayne was married. She hoped Wayne would divorce his wife and marry her when the baby was born. Alberto remembered when Lupe gave him the two keys and told him to hide them in a safe place in the back of the building. "In case of an emergency," she said. Alberto understood that Lupe was worried about getting locked out by Wayne one day. If that happened, she could use the hidden keys to go back in and get Wayne's money. Alberto found a loose brick near the back entrance and hid the keys there. Later he showed Lupe the hiding place so she too would know. The key to the front also opened the door in the back used by the super to take out the trash. He would go in that way and then make his way up the emergency stairs. It was unlikely for Wayne to be there at this hour, but he would be cautious. He would listen at the door of the apartment and make sure he did not hear Wayne's voice before he opened it.

Get Wayne's money. You know where it is.

Would I lie to you?

Alberto reached the corner of the street and stood behind a light post. Wayne's black SUV was not parked anywhere on the street. Alberto watched the cars in front of Lupe's apartment to see if any of them were occupied. They were all empty. He waited a few more minutes and then walked toward the apartment building with his head down. He crossed the street and entered the alley that would take him to the back of Lupe's building. He found the brick, dislodged it, and took out the keys. Then he opened the back door a crack and peeked to make sure Mr. Romulo, the super, was not in the garbage room. There was no one. He entered and quickly made his way to the stairs. He ran up to the fourth floor. The only two tenants who ever used the stairs were Alberto and Officer Ramos, the policeman who lived in 3D. Officer Ramos once told Alberto, as they were walking up the stairs, that his dog did not like the elevator.

The dog, a pit bull, licked Alberto's hand, and Officer Ramos said, looking carefully at Alberto, that his dog had never licked anyone other than him, his wife, and his kids. Alberto wondered whether the same dog would lick his hand now.

Alberto opened the door to the fourth floor just a crack. He had a clear view of Lupe's apartment. He was digging in his pocket for the keys when he saw the door to Lupe's apartment open. He heard Lupe's voice. Inside the apartment, baby Chato was crying. Alberto was about to step out into the hall when Lucas exited the apartment. Alberto froze. His first thought, when he was thinking again, was of rushing out, tackling Lucas, getting on top of him, and beating his face with his fists until all the bones were mush.

Now you're talking!

Grace was in the school library using one of the computers. She searched for Ticul in Wikipedia. Knowing where he was from was going to help her get some needed closure on Alberto. She would see what she already knew—that their worlds were too distant and too different to ever meet. Alberto had said that his family had moved from a small town to the city of Ticul, and she had imagined a big city, but Ticul had twenty-nine thousand inhabitants—that was about how many people lived in ten blocks of Manhattan. She smiled when she read that the city was known for its red-clay pottery. She clicked on a website with pictures of the city. There was a picture of a young boy sitting on the ground making a large planter in front of him. The boy was barefoot and was wearing a T-shirt with the image of an electric guitar. She tried to remember everything that Alberto had said to her about his life. It wasn't very much. He was trying to get his high school equivalency. He read books on Japanese pottery making. He lived with his sister in John Wayne's apartment. The name of his sister's baby, did Alberto ever say what it was?

"You plan on visiting Mexico?" Michael had come up behind her and was looking at the picture on the screen.

She minimized the window. "Hi," she said.

Michael pulled out the chair next to her and sat down. He had two paper cups with coffee. He offered her one. "It's from the machine at the cafeteria. You get here early?"

"Makeup exam. Physics. I thought I'd get it over with."

"How'd you do?"

Grace shrugged. "So-so."

"I'm sure you aced it."

Grace detected a slight tone of hurt in Michael's words. She watched him take a deep breath. He was having trouble saying whatever was on his mind. Finally, Grace said, "Listen, I'm sorry about last night. You guys were so nice to come over and bring dinner, and I was so . . ."

"Ungrateful?" Michael volunteered.

The word and the quickness with which it came stung Grace. "Really?" she asked, trying to dampen the anger she felt rising.

"You receive the highest academic honor that this school can give and you're, like, complaining about it?"

"I'm not sure I was complaining."

"You weren't appreciative."

Grace nodded. Michael was right. She was not being appreciative. Something had happened to the appreciation she had for the good things in her life. It was a momentary condition, wasn't it? "Michael . . ."

"Let me just say what I need to say."

"It sounds serious. Maybe this isn't the right time." Grace reached out and held his hand. Michael pulled it away.

"The other morning . . . last Sunday when I came over, I'm not sure I fully understood the extent of your doubts."

"Oh, Michael. Do you really want to go there? I don't have it all together right now. I seem to be going through some . . . questioning. It's not just you."

"It hit me last night after we left your valedictorian celebration that if two people love each other and one of them is going through a period of . . . questioning, as you put it, they would share their questioning with the person they love."

Grace rubbed her temples. She didn't need this conversation. For one, she wasn't sure she could find the right words. "It was just . . . I needed some time."

"You think I'm too insensitive to understand?"

"No."

"It hurts, Grace! It hurts to be lumped in with all the things you're questioning."

Four students at a nearby table turned to look at them.

When Michael spoke again, his voice was softer. "I can feel you pushing me away."

"I know." He was right. Whether deliberate or not, the effect of all her actions was to push him away. "I see how you could feel that way."

"And now you're, what? Looking up Mexico? Really? The window washer? You're in touch with him?"

Grace raised the palm of her hand. "You don't need to go there, please."

Michael grimaced with pain, as if Grace's words had affirmatively answered his question. "What should I do, Grace? Something, someone's come between us. Please don't deny that."

Grace thought for a moment. Now was the moment when she should reach out and hold Michael's hand and tell him he was the one she chose. This was the time to say I love you. And it would be true. She did love him. Of course. Only, why couldn't she get the words out? "I . . . yes, you're right. I pushed you away somehow. I didn't even know I was doing it. I, uh, it felt like something I needed to do."

"What's going on with you and this . . . boy from Mexico?"

Grace hesitated in responding. It seemed like an inappropriate question. Or maybe it was Michael's tone, as if he deserved an answer, that irritated her. She waited for the rising anger to subside. "I saw him yesterday. He was in trouble and I helped him."

"What kind of trouble?"

"Someone beat him up."

"Is that all?"

"Are you interrogating me?"

"I was sitting with my father last night to discuss my summer plans when who should appear on the news but the picture of your Mexican friend. Grace, you need to know, he's a person of interest on a murder—"

"Alberto. Alberto is his name."

Michael closed his eyes. He reached out and held on to Grace's hand. "Gracie, don't throw away your future, our future, like this. You get caught helping this guy and . . ."

"I know. I know."

"Helping this guy is just a way to feel better about yourself. You're going through a hard phase in your life, and here comes someone you can save. Now suddenly you like yourself again. Can't you see what's happening? Please tell me you're not going to see him again."

Grace giggled.

"You find my request humorous?"

"I'm sorry. I was laughing at myself. When I set out to school this morning, I wanted to do three things: take the physics test, talk to you, and put Alberto behind me."

"Good."

"But if it's good, why do I feel like a coward? Why do

I feel like someone who needed me called my name and I hid under the bed? The thought of helping him is not making me feel better about myself. The opposite. I see who I am and what I have and I'm terrified of losing it."

"Because you have a good heart. That's who you are." Michael leaned over, lifted Grace's chin, and kissed her softly on the lips. "I gotta go. Listen, I'll be at the club tomorrow morning playing in the Holbrook Tournament. It will mean a lot to me if you come. It will be a sign to me that you believe in our future. Hey, you know how much winning that means to me. I want you to be a part of that. We can go to the city afterward. Have lunch. Walk around. Talk."

"Okay."

Grace watched Michael walk out of the library. When he was gone, she raised the fingers of her right hand to her lips. She remembered the kiss she gave Alberto. How was it different from Michael's? The touch of the flesh had been the same, but there was music, beautiful and sad, in Alberto's lips.

Alberto waited until his anger at seeing Lucas in Lupe's apartment had passed. He tried to understand why Lucas's presence made him so angry. He did not like

Lucas, that was true. Lucas was a jerk. And now Alberto knew for sure that Lucas had been supplying Lupe with drugs all along. Alberto remembered Lupe saying that she had a plan to leave Wayne. Lucas was her plan.

Your sister is a parasite.

Lucas shouted: "Come on! Let's hurry it up! You can finish packing later." A few seconds later, Lupe came out with baby Chato crying in her arms. Lupe looked like her old drug-addict self. There were dark circles under her eyes and her hair was unwashed. She was wearing a black halter top, jeans, and silver sneakers that were untied. She closed the door and then reached out and clumsily kissed Lucas's neck.

"Thank you!" she mumbled. "I always hated this place."

They walked toward the elevator side by side, Lupe with baby Chato on her hip. Lupe's left hand was shaking uncontrollably, her head bobbing from side to side—signs that she had been using heroin.

Kill them both! They don't deserve to live!

"And baby Chato?" Alberto whispered.

The rage that had filled him when he first saw Lucas turned into sorrow. Lupe's return to addiction meant she had turned away from him, her family, her blood.

I told you about your sister. Didn't I tell you?

Alberto ran down the stairs, out the back door, and through the alley. He was in time to see Lupe get into the front seat of a yellow Toyota with baby Chato on her lap. Lucas helped Lupe with the seat belt so that it went across baby Chato and then walked over to the driver's side and got in. Alberto went back through the alley and up the stairs to Lupe's apartment.

There were boxes and plastic bags with Lupe's clothes all over the living room. *Lupe's leaving Wayne to be with Lucas.* Lupe's phone was on the kitchen table. He tapped Lupe's password, *Chato 1,* and checked Lupe's history of phone calls. There were numerous calls to a phone number he recognized as Lucas's. The phone calls had started in early April, almost two months ago. He tore a corner from a magazine page and wrote down Lucas's number.

It was strange that Lupe and Lucas would be so open about their relationship. What if Wayne showed up? Alberto walked to Lupe's bedroom and opened Wayne's closet. His clothes were all gone. He opened the dresser drawer where Wayne kept his underwear and saw that it was empty. He walked down to the bedroom that Wayne used for an office, and the desktop computer and printer were no longer there. It was Wayne who left Lupe and now wanted her out. Was it because of Lucas?

Alberto went back to Lupe's bedroom and searched behind a pile of dirty clothes until he found the shoe where Lupe had hidden the combination to Wayne's safe. He entered the numbers in the keypad and opened the safe. The safe was empty. Of course; Wayne would not leave without his money. Why did Lupe think that Alberto had stolen the money? Alberto looked again and saw the Captain America comic book. Alberto took the comic out and closed the safe again.

Check the floorboard in your closet.

Alberto made his way to his room. He placed the comic book on his desk and then stood over the open door to the closet, staring at the clothes on the floor. It looked as if every single item in his chest of drawers had been dumped there. He moved sweatshirts and pants out of the way and found a loose nail, which he used to lift the board. He stuck his hand in carefully and then quickly took it out when he touched the cold metal of Wayne's gun. After a few moments, he reached in again and pulled out a plastic bag with a dozen or so one-hundred-dollar bills. He lay facedown on the floor and searched around the floor cavity as far as his arms would go, until his fingers brushed something cold. He grabbed it and pulled out a gold coin. A gold coin he must have taken from Mrs. Macpherson's apartment after he killed her.

Now he knew.

He sat on the edge of his bed and let the salty water run down his cheeks. He didn't even call it crying anymore. How he felt when tears rolled out was only slightly different from when they didn't.

"I killed her."

What I tell you?

When the tears stopped, he counted the bills. There were only seventeen one-hundred-dollar bills. That was not even close to the forty thousand that Lupe had told him was in the safe. He waited to hear the familiar voice.

You hid the rest!

"Where?"

How the hell should I know?

"Where are the rest of Mrs. Macpherson's things? Did I only steal one coin?"

I don't keep track of what you forget!

Alberto sat at his desk with pencil and paper and proceeded to calculate how much money Wayne owed him. Alberto figured that by paying him seven dollars per hour instead of the fifteen he paid Lucas and Jimbo,

Wayne owed him approximately ten thousand dollars. Alberto put the seventeen bills in his backpack. It wasn't close to ten thousand dollars, but it would do. He placed the gun and the gold coin back in the hole and closed it with the board. He hit the nail with a shoe and moved the clothes the way they were before. He took one last look at his room. The bed was unmade and a spiderweb hung in a corner of the ceiling. Lupe was right. At some point he had stopped caring about cleanliness and order. It was the room of a killer and a thief.

Grace skipped all her morning classes and stayed in the library. For a while she tried to understand what had happened with Michael. They'd almost broken up, but he'd given her another chance. Why did she feel once again as if she had acted without choosing to act? But she had chosen. She had chosen to cut herself off from Alberto. That was the right decision even if she felt like she was circling around in a drain that had just been unplugged.

The bell for lunch period had rung and Grace had not heard it. Students were eating or talking quietly or on their phones. Lunch period was the only time that Mrs. Barnes permitted food in the library. Grace's phone buzzed. It was Ernestina's number. She picked up her backpack and walked outside.

"Hi, Ernestina," Grace said when she was outside the library.

"It's me, Joseph. Gracie, have you heard from Alberto this morning?"

"No, what happened?"

"He spent the night at the synagogue, but he was gone this morning."

"Oh!" Grace sat on a ledge.

"I had a visit from a Detective Lydell of the NYPD last evening around seven. She was certain I was hiding Alberto. I let her walk through the house even though she didn't have a warrant, just to get rid of her, but how did she know?"

Grace was shaken by guilt of not telling Joseph about Alberto's alleged crime. "Joseph . . ."

Joseph continued, his words coming out fast, "This Detective Lydell is convinced Alberto killed the woman. I asked her if she had a warrant for his arrest and she said she was waiting for lab results on blood they found on his shirt to come in. She said the other two working with Alberto had alibis. The woman was alive when the other two were back home and they can prove it. The time of the woman's death corresponds to when Alberto was the only one there. I managed to get all that out of her in case it could help Alberto, but there wasn't much that was helpful."

"I should have told you . . . about the police," Grace said meekly.

"Grace, I hope you become a regular part of our lives, mine, Benny's, Ernestina's, but if you do, you need to know that being honest with each other is important to us. Do you understand?"

"Yes."

"Good."

"I'm sorry."

"No need to talk about it anymore."

After a long pause, Grace asked, "Do you think he did it?"

"My heart says no. And then there is this: Benny took to him like a brother, and Benny can see into a person's soul."

Grace wished her heart was as confident of Alberto's innocence as Joseph's. "Maybe he wasn't himself. The voice he hears."

"Rabbi Sacks believes Alberto has a strong sense of self, despite the voice. But even the strongest tree eventually falls to a small ax. He needs help. If you hear from him, tell him to go back to the synagogue where he spent the night. Ernestina tells me there's a police car in front of the house. Are you all right, Grace?"

"Yes. I'm going home now. I'll wait for his call."

Grace stared at her phone. What would she say to Alberto if he called? *Turn yourself in. We'll get you a lawyer. I'm so sorry. There's nothing more I can do.* It was better not to say anything.

Grace turned her phone off and began her walk home.

CHAPTER 19

Alberto found an alley behind the bodega where he bought a disposable phone and a prepaid phone card for Mexico. He tapped the number for Mercedes's cell phone.

"Is everything all right?" Mercedes asked, when she found out it was Alberto. "We've been calling and calling Lupe, and no one answers."

"Why? Is something wrong?"

"Mami is sick. We took her to the doctor. He said it could be pneumonia. We got medicine. We rented an oxygen tank. He didn't want to send her to the hospital.

You know, the hospital here is only a way station to the cemetery."

"Did Lupe send you the money for this month?"

"No. We got the medicines on credit. Where is Lupe? What's happening, Beto?"

"In a few minutes I will send you one thousand five hundred dollars. You can pick it up later today at the bank. Use it for Mamá and make it last. I don't know when I will be able to send you money again. Lupe . . . is using again."

"Oh my God. And the baby?"

"I don't know what to do about Chatito."

"You come home. Bring Lupe and the baby if you can. Or just the baby if you can't get Lupe to come. Don Andrés will give you your job back. I can work at the brewery."

"You're going to be a doctor, hermanita. I wish I could be there to see it."

"Why can't you? Please come home, Beto, you're scaring me."

"I have to go. Dile a Mamá que la quiero más que el mar."

Alberto stared at the phone for a few moments and then made one more call. Lupe might be a drug addict, but she was also a mother. Alberto thought of pleading with her to think of Chatito. He would tell her about their sick mother. Lupe was a good person. Beneath the hungers of addiction, she was good. No one answered. Alberto called again and left a message.

"Call me at this number. Please. We need to find a way to keep Chatito safe. He's not safe with Lucas. I know you're with him. Por favor, Lupe, be a mother."

Alberto walked in the direction of the shops at the end of the street. What could he do about Chatito? The only thing he could think was that Ernestina and Joseph and the kind rabbi would help. On the following block Alberto found a pawnshop where he sent the fifteen hundred dollars to Mercedes. He was about to leave when he saw the comic books at the front counter. He took out the Captain America comic book from his backpack and showed it to the man working there. The man examined it carefully. He made a face as if to indicate that the comic book was worthless. Alberto was placing the comic book in the backpack when the man said: "I'll give you fifty for it."

Alberto was about to give the man the comic book when he heard a voice.

"May I?" A man with red hair, about twenty years

old, took the comic book from Alberto's hand and shook his head. He looked up at the man behind the counter. "Fifty dollars? You can't be serious. How do you sleep at night?"

"All right. Two hundred," the man said.

The man, Alberto noticed, had very thick glasses and his hair had tinges of purple. He had the body of an adult but the freckled face of a young boy. The man tapped his phone for a few moments. "Look at this." He turned the phone in the direction first of Alberto and then of the pawnshop man and showed them a picture of the very same comic book that Alberto held in his hand. "See this? It's Captain America punching Hitler, the 1941 first issue of the Captain America comics." The man clicked the image off and said to Alberto, "Let's get out of here."

"One thousand dollars," the pawnshop man shouted as they stepped out.

"Listen," the man said, "it's obvious you don't know much about vintage comic books, do you?"

You know nothing about nothing!

"No."

"This comic belongs to you, right? You didn't steal it or anything."

You stole it!

"It belongs to me."

"And you want to sell it."

It's not yours to sell.

"My family in Mexico needs money."

"Okay, okay. This is what I'm thinking. The way to get the most out of this comic book is to auction it. I can do that for you. I'll take some pictures of it and put them up on the sites where comic book connoisseurs go. I'll sell it for you. Handle everything. All you need to do is hold on to the comic book until I tell you. And in return I get, I don't know, ten percent?"

Alberto had read about percentages in the high school equivalency books, but at that moment he could not remember how they worked.

The man continued quickly, "If I sell it for ten thousand dollars, let's say, then you get nine thousand and I get one thousand."

"What's your name?" Alberto asked.

"Andy. Andy Margulies. What do you think?"

"Where do you live?"

Andy pointed at the twelve-story building across the street. "Right there. Apartment 3B."

Alberto took out the comic book and placed it on the hood of a white car. "Go ahead, take pictures."

"Really? We got a deal?"

"Yes. We got a deal. Do you have a pen and a piece of paper? I'll give you an address."

While Andy took pictures of the front, the back, and some of the inner pages of the comic book, Alberto wrote on the piece of paper that Andy had given to him. Andy placed the comic book back inside the plastic bag. He was about to give it back when Alberto said, "Keep it."

"What?"

You are worse than a moron.

"Sell it and then send the money to my sister in Mexico. Minus your ten percent. Here's her name and address and her phone. Call her today and tell her what you're doing with the comic book. Then when you sell it, she'll tell you how to send the money to a bank in Ticul. That's where she lives. Ticul, Yucatán, Mexico. I'll call and tell her to expect your call."

"But . . . you don't even know me."

You're an ass.

"I heard you ask the man in there how he could sleep at night . . . when he was trying to cheat me. I think you're

honest. Also, I know where you live, Andy Margulies."
Alberto moved closer and glared.

"Yeah." Andy daintily touched the muscle on Alberto's left arm. "Don't worry. I'm very honest, especially when I fear for my life."

"You give me your word?" Alberto looked into Andy's eyes.

"Word." Andy extended his hand and Alberto took it. "Wait, where you going to be? Is there a way to reach you?"

Alberto handed him his phone and Andy typed a number. When Andy was finished, Alberto took the phone and dropped it in his backpack. "Be nice to my sister," he said, walking away.

You are going to die.

Grace heard her mother's voice just before she opened the door to her apartment. Her mother and Detective Lydell were sitting across from each other on the kitchen table. Detective Lydell had a glass of water in front of her. Grace noticed that the glass did not have any ice cubes. They both rose when Grace entered and waited for Grace to drop her backpack next to the door.

"You've met Detective Lydell," Miriam said.

Grace nodded. She pulled out a chair next to her mother. The angry glare on Detective Lydell's face made Grace's heart race, and perspiration popped up on her forehead. "What happened? Did something happen?"

"I was just telling Detective Lydell about how our jobs have similar stress levels," Miriam said, looking at Detective Lydell.

Detective Lydell directed her words at Grace. She was barely able to contain her anger. "Yesterday morning, you went to see Alberto Bocel at the pottery shop and then, according to the owner, you and Bocel took a taxi. The records from the taxi company indicate you went to your grandfather's house. You did this after I had specifically told you to call me the next time you heard from him. I am this close to charging you with interfering with a police investigation. This close." Detective Lydell brought her thumb and finger up to Grace's face.

"No threats, please." Miriam's voice was calm but firm.

"Where is he?" Detective Lydell asked, ignoring Miriam.

"I don't know," Grace said. She wished she could say that again, this time without the fear in her voice.

Detective Lydell opened the notepad and read. "Carol Jennings, the owner of the pottery studio across the park, called you yesterday at 8:15 a.m. and told you Bocel was hurt, a mugging maybe. You went to see him. There was time for you to call me. Why didn't you?"

"Detective, watch the tone," Miriam warned.

"He was hurt. Would you have given him the kind of help he needed?" Grace felt her strength start to flow back.

Detective Lydell grinned. "I'm going to ask again. Where is he?"

"I'm going to say again, I don't know."

"Where did he spend the night? Where did he go after he left your grandfather's house? Yeah, I know he took off just before I got there. There were still indentations on a living room chair."

"I don't know where he went. He was only going to stay at my grandfather's for a while. He planned to leave again when it was dark. Why do you think he's guilty? You said he was a person of interest. Aren't you required to presume someone's innocent until proven guilty?"

Detective Lydell looked surprised at Grace's questioning. "I'm getting a warrant for his arrest tomorrow morning. If I don't have one now it's because the lab's backed up."

"What makes you think this boy did it?" Miriam asked calmly.

"That's irrelevant to why I'm here," Detective Lydell responded, annoyed.

"I don't know," Miriam mused. "I think it's important for us to know—to better answer your questions."

"We got the victim's blood on his shirt and his fingerprints on the doorknob to her room. We got her time of death almost to the minute and the two other workers were not there when she died." Detective Lydell looked at Grace. "After he killed the old woman, he stole forty thousand dollars and a gun from his employer, the man who owned the apartment where he lived. His own sister testified to that," Detective Lydell said with an air of triumph.

"How was the woman killed?" Grace asked, afraid to hear the answer.

"Blunt force trauma to the head. Her skull caved in with a candlestick that's missing," Detective Lydell snapped.

"Has an autopsy been done?" Miriam asked.

"Look," Detective Lydell said, "the boy has enough money to take a bus back to Mexico. That's why we have to move fast. Not to mention the fact that he's running and hiding from us and your daughter is helping him." Lydell drank the water in her glass and stood. She spoke to Grace: "If you continue to lie to me, I'll haul you in for aiding and abetting, obstruction, and whatever else I can think of."

"I think you've overstayed your welcome, Detective," Miriam said coldly. "There's the door."

"All right, all right. Apologies. It's been a rough day, a rough week." Detective Lydell sat down again. "Grace, I know you don't believe me, but finding him is for his own good. There's an armed and dangerous BOLO on him, and who knows what can happen when we try to apprehend someone who is armed."

"BOLO?" Grace asked.

"Be on the lookout." Detective Lydell paused for a moment. "Is there anything you can tell me? Any plans he shared with you as to where he might go, or as to what he wanted to do?"

"Jim . . ." Grace stopped herself. What was she doing? Was she going to tell Detective Lydell what Alberto shared with her? It was for his own good, wasn't it?

"Jimbo? What about Jimbo?" Detective Lydell guessed what Grace had begun to say.

"He talked about finding Jimbo. Alberto thought Jimbo could . . . help him. Help him prove his innocence."

"He believes he's innocent," Miriam repeated to Detective Lydell.

"People lie," Detective Lydell said to Miriam. Then, to Grace, "Does he know where Jimbo lives?"

Grace shook her head. "He was going to go look for him, try to find where he lives." She stopped herself from telling Detective Lydell about the church where Jimbo's mother worked. At least she didn't completely feed Alberto to the wolf.

"Okay. Now, please call me if you hear anything." Detective Lydell nodded in Miriam's direction and then opened the door. She turned to Grace before stepping out. "His sister showed me a picture of Bocel. He's hot. Agree?"

Grace shrugged and said, "Not my type."

Detective Lydell grinned and then stepped out.

Miriam waited a few moments and then got up and locked the door to the apartment. "What an obnoxious woman."

"Did I do the right thing? Telling her about where Alberto might be?"

Miriam filled a wineglass from a bottle of Chardonnay in the refrigerator. She then came and sat next to Grace.

"That policewoman may have been nasty, but she was also smart. She wanted to see if there was some kind of bond between you and Alberto."

"Bond? I don't know the meaning of the word. Alberto trusted me for some reason, and what do I do?"

"Don't be hard on yourself. We will do all we can to help him. He really is better off not running. He will be well represented, I assure you."

"That detective seems so sure Alberto did it. She's not looking into other possibilities. What if the other workers killed the woman? Do people die immediately from blunt force trauma? The woman could have been hit and died later."

"Good point," Miriam said. Then: "Will you see him again?"

Grace shut her eyes for a few moments. When she opened them again, she said, "I know where I can find Alberto tomorrow. If I go meet him, I can try to help him, however I can. Should I do that?"

"I think you know a mother's answer to that question."

Grace ignored her mother's words and continued, "If I see Alberto, Michael will probably break up with me."

"He told you that?"

"In so many words. I don't want to lose Michael."

Miriam grabbed both sides of her head, exasperated. "Men and their fragile, oversize egos. What the hell's the matter with them?"

"What would you do, Mom, if you were in my place?"

Miriam thought for a few moments. Gulped down the white wine remaining in her glass. "I'm not you, Grace. You'll have to decide. You told me a few days ago that it didn't feel as if you had chosen your future. Well, here's a choice you need to make."

"Choosing is not what it's cracked up to be," Grace said, smiling. She stood and walked to the living room window. Out in the park, a little girl and her father were flying a kite in the shape of a blue butterfly.

CHAPTER 20

Alberto arrived at Our Lady of the Presentation church just as the sun was coming up. He had spent the night in the basement of Lupe's apartment building. There was a room where Mr. Romulo kept tools and cleaning supplies that Alberto found open. There, with a bag of sand for a pillow, he had tried unsuccessfully to sleep. It wasn't just Captain America's constant remarks. It was not knowing what to do next. If he'd killed Mrs. Macpherson, then he should turn himself over to the police. What was he waiting for? Didn't the money and the gun under his closet prove his guilt beyond doubt? He didn't remember killing

Mrs. Macpherson and he didn't remember taking Wayne's money and gun, and there were other unknowns, like what happened to the rest of Wayne's money, but so what. Hadn't he seen his memory falter many times in the past few weeks? A few times, he took out his phone and was ready to dial 911. What stopped him? The thought of seeing Grace one more time? In Grace's message to Ernestina, Grace said that she would come. What would he say to her? He would tell her all he'd found out. Then he would say goodbye to her. Turn himself in.

Turning yourself in is not the only option.

The other option, the one that Captain America had repeated all night like a hammer on an anvil, was simpler and had the added benefit of silencing Captain America forever. It was strange that Captain America wanted Alberto to die. Wouldn't that end him as well?

"You want to die because you're guilty. It's you that should be punished. It wasn't me that killed Mrs. Macpherson. It was you. You used my hands to kill her," Alberto shouted to Captain America.

Captain America didn't answer.

Grace sat on a bleacher overlooking the main tennis court of the Steward Johnson Country Club. Michael's first match, she saw on a bulletin board, would not be for another hour. All night long her heart had waged battle against her head, and in the end her head won. She surrendered to the easiest, less complicated, safest path. She was choosing by not choosing. It all came down to the clarity she knew versus the mystery she didn't. She could see the future with Michael. Alberto was a bad *now* and an even worse *tomorrow*. The head won. Now there she was, waiting for Michael and feeling ashamed.

Stella told her once that, according to her mother, when we die, we are led to a big theater where we get to see the movie of our life. Everything we did will be replayed, including very private stuff. Then when the movie is over, the dead person, on her own, decides which way to go. Up or down. The biggest concern for Stella had been who else would be in the theater when her movie was played. If it was just an angel and her, it wouldn't be so bad. But what if people like her grandmother were there?

Grace was thinking that she wouldn't want to watch the movie showing the moment she was living, when her cell phone buzzed. It was Joseph's number. She held the vibrating phone in her hand. What if it was Alberto calling her? What would she say? *I'm so sorry but I can't be involved with someone who hears voices and is wanted for*

murder. Please, you must understand, those kinds of prob-
lems are more than I can handle. I'm so sorry. She covered
her face and waited for the phone to stop ringing. When
the phone went silent, she noticed that her hands were
wet with sweat. She checked her messages, but there
were none. Then the phone rang again. The same
number. *Why are you so insistent? Leave me alone.* The
memory of the kiss came to her. Alberto's closed eyes. It
was like sinking into tenderness, like finding shade on a
blistering day. On the sixth ring, Grace answered.

"Hello."

"This is Benny Reuben. Your cousin." The voice still
had remnants of a child's voice, but the tone was mature.

"Benny! How nice to hear from you! I'm sorry I didn't
get to see you yesterday."

"Yes, unfortunately I was in school."

"Is everything all right?"

"No, not really. I never make phone calls on the
Sabbath, but this is an emergency. Ernestina said you
gave her an address to give to Alberto. Unfortunately,
Ernestina doesn't remember the address. She wrote it
down on a note card and gave it to Alberto. All she can
remember is that it was a church. Do you still have the
address? I need to find Alberto."

"Why? Why do you need to find him?"

There was a long silence during which Grace felt very stupid.

"He's all alone with that voice. I don't want him to be alone."

Benny sounded as if he had been asked why people need to eat.

Tears filled Grace's eyes. She held her cell phone against her chest. She wished Benny had never called. His courage shone a bright light on her cowardice. After a long while, she looked at her phone and saw that Benny was still on the line. "Hi. Sorry. I needed a moment."

"I could hear you crying," Benny said. "You care about Alberto, don't you?"

"Yes. But obviously not enough to help him the way you want to."

"I understand," Benny said. "You're afraid that maybe he killed that woman. Or maybe you're afraid of the voice he hears."

"And you're not?" Grace asked.

"Of course I am."

"But you're still willing to be with him?"

"He's my friend."

"But you've only known him for a couple of hours." Grace wiped the tears from her eyes.

"You are saying some very silly things, Grace. My friend Samuel didn't even meet Alberto, and he's agreed to help me find him. Being with Alberto is what we're asked to do. We are Jews. When the Holy One asks us for our help, we say yes."

Grace saw a tennis player warming up on the court below. The girl was practicing backhands and forehands and imaginary serves. All the girl's movements were precise and elegant and they reminded Grace of a theatrical performance for the benefit of no one. At that moment, Grace felt as if a veil lifted and she could see, for the first time, how much she was needed.

"Grace? Are you still there?"

"Benny, listen, I'll tell you what. I'll go look for Alberto at that address I gave Ernestina and if I find him, I'll bring him to you and Joseph or I'll find a way to be with him so he's not alone."

"Really, you'll do that?"

"Yes . . . I'll try." Grace could hear the fear in her voice.

"Grace, it's okay to be afraid. Rabbi Sacks says that

courage is like a winter coat. You put it on and it's only after a while it begins to warm you. You're not warm before you put it on. You get it?"

"I think I do. How did you get so wise for a kid?"

"I'm twelve years old. And I read a lot."

Grace laughed.

"Will you look for Alberto and keep looking until you find him?"

Somewhere, deep in her, Grace found a very frightened yes.

The inside of Our Lady of the Presentation church was cheery, with a blue carpet and a brightly lit white altar. The smell of gardenias and the statute of the Virgin Mary reminded Alberto of the church in Ticul. He had sat through Sunday Mass with his mother, wishing he was back home with his father. Still, it was peaceful to be in a place where people prayed. The church was empty except for a man kneeling in the front pew, his head bowed. There was no sign of anyone who looked like she could be Mrs. Jasmine, so Alberto decided to go outside and wait. From the front steps of the church, he saw a small park with a couple of wooden benches. From there he could watch the church and wait for Mrs. Jasmine.

Alberto had to sit on the edge of the bench and turn sideways to observe the entrance to the church. The small park where he was sitting was an island of green in a sea of concrete and noise. Once, it was not hard for him to find an island like that inside his mind. Not anymore. He was surrounded by Captain America and painful thoughts. There was Lupe's addiction and baby Chato's care. There was his sick mother at home.

Sitting on the bench, the green wooden slabs wet with dew, Alberto now regretted dragging Grace into his mess. What was he thinking when he called out her name that morning at the pottery studio? Yet here he was wishing to see her again.

You want to screw the girl.

It hurt him to hear those words from Captain America. It made what he felt for Grace seem vulgar and dirty.

You want to screw her.

"No, you lie. Nothing is possible between us. Even my friendship will hurt her. I want to say goodbye to her, thank her. That is all I'm going to say or think about this. I'm not going to talk to you anymore."

She'll be better off when you're dead.

"Probably."

You have only one option.

Sometimes Captain America spoke and sometimes Captain America put thoughts in his head. Captain America wanted Alberto to fight the tall man from the back of Rabbi Sacks's church and ask if he could join his group. Surely, they could use a fighter and a killer like him. That was one option. The second option, and the one Captain America preferred, was to let the tall man kill him.

Alberto turned to see Grace step out of the back seat of a green taxi in front of the church. When the car pulled away, Grace looked around. Alberto's first instinct was to lower his head and hide behind the bench, but that felt like a cowardly thing to do. He stood and waited for Grace to look in his direction. He responded to Grace's wave by lifting his hand.

Go ahead. Have a little fun with the bitch.

Grace ran across Saint Mark's Avenue when there was an opening in the flow of cars. She was out of breath when she entered the park. She stopped a few feet in front of him and then walked up and hugged him. It was an awkward hug, with Alberto's lips momentarily touching the top of Grace's head, but it was enough for Alberto to feel what he had felt all night.

Grace pulled herself away from Alberto when she felt him wince. "Sorry, I forgot about your ribs."

"No, I'm okay." Alberto placed his hand first on his chest and then below on his abdomen. "It doesn't hurt so much."

Grace brushed a strand of hair from her face. She didn't know where to put her hands. She tried tucking them in the pockets of her jeans. It might have been a mistake to hug him. She had been nervous on the way, but it was nothing compared to this wild pounding of her heart. "Did you check to see if Mrs. Jasmine is in the church?" she asked.

"Who?"

"Mrs. Jasmine. Jimbo's mother."

"No . . . I haven't seen . . . anyone," Alberto stammered. He had forgotten the original reason for coming to the church.

Grace turned her head and saw the red doors of the church. She sat on the bench and when Alberto had done the same, she said: "I wasn't going to come. I had decided not to . . . and then I got a call from Benny about half an hour ago. He wanted to come find you. Because he didn't want you to be alone. Because you were his friend."

"Benny said he was my friend?" Alberto asked.

"Yes!"

Alberto's face broke into a big smile, as if knowing that made all kinds of things better.

"Alberto, you know what I've been thinking?" Grace didn't give Alberto an opportunity to respond. "The other workers. Jimbo and the other guy."

"Lucas."

"Lucas. I know they weren't there when the woman died. But the whole thing hasn't been investigated properly. Detective Lydell came to our apartment yesterday and told us that the woman died from blunt force trauma, from a blow to the head. But then after she left I did some research on blunt force trauma to the head and found that death can result an hour or two after the incident."

"You did research? You were worried about me?"

Grace did not tell Alberto that the research was to make her feel less guilty for telling Detective Lydell where she could find him. Grace went on, "What if Mrs. Macpherson was hit in the head while Jimbo and Lucas were there but she didn't *die* until later? How does Lydell know for sure she died of blunt force trauma when no autopsy has been performed?" Grace turned sideways so

(246)

she could see the entrance to the church. She told herself to slow down. No need to talk a mile a minute. Act normal, if possible.

Alberto tried to listen to Grace, but he was distracted by a ray of sunlight streaming through the branches and lighting Grace's face. How beautiful she was.

Grace lost her train of thought. No one had ever looked at her with that mixture of intensity and gentleness. It was as if Alberto could not believe she was real.

"What?" she said, looking away, embarrassed.

"You came all the way here for me? You came even after the police came to see you in your home."

"I almost didn't."

Alberto smiled. He understood. Then he said, "They also think I stole Wayne's money and his gun, but I don't remember doing it. He had them in a safe in Lupe's bedroom. Yesterday I went to the apartment and looked in a hiding place no one knew about but me, and some of the money and the gun were there. There was also a gold coin that must have belonged to Mrs. Macpherson. That I don't remember doing bad things doesn't mean I didn't do them."

Alberto's words stunned Grace. His words said he was a killer, but his eyes, everything else about him, said he wasn't. Her heart did not believe his words. Then the last words he said triggered a question in her mind. "Some of the money?"

"Wayne had forty thousand when Lupe showed me Wayne's safe a long time ago, but there was only one thousand seven hundred in my hiding place."

"And where's the rest of the money? If you took it, where is it? And what about the other things stolen from Mrs. Macpherson?"

"I don't remember."

"How can you not remember that? It's not something one forgets." Grace almost shook him. "Alberto, can there be another explanation for how the money and the gun and the coin got there? Maybe you're too quick to blame yourself."

Shut her up!

Alberto grabbed his ears and grimaced.

"The voice?" Grace asked.

"It takes so much more now to ignore it. I feel like there's less and less willingness in me to resist. It's like I'm holding on to the edge of a cliff. How long can I hold on? Soon I will need to let go."

"You need to go to a safe place where people who know about voices can help you."

Alberto continued, lost in thought. "Yesterday I went to Lupe's apartment. I saw her. It looked like she was moving out of the apartment and going to live with Lucas. She's back on heroin. She was with Lucas. She got into his car, a yellow Toyota Corolla, with baby Chato. I found Lucas's phone number in her phone. They have been in touch for the last two months. I didn't know, but Lucas has been giving Lupe drugs for a while."

"Alberto, is it possible that Lucas stole Wayne's money, took most of it, and left enough for you to be blamed? If Lupe is ill with addiction and needed money, isn't it possible that she told him about Wayne's money?"

"No one but me knew about my hiding place."

"But it's possible that Lupe found it and didn't tell you, isn't it? It's possible."

You stole the money. I saw you.

"Lupe may be a drug addict . . . but she is family. She's my sister. She wouldn't do that." Alberto remembered when Pilar accused Lupe of stealing jewelry from her and then, later, Alberto had found Pilar's bracelet in Lupe's things.

"What about Lucas?"

"Lucas . . . he is mean . . . sometimes he wants to steal from the apartments we paint but Jimbo stops him."

Grace grabbed Alberto's chin and lifted his head until their eyes met. "Listen, let's assume you didn't kill Mrs. Macpherson. If you didn't kill her, then somebody else had to do it."

"I was there when she died. They found her blood on my shirt. My fingerprints on the doorknob."

"Alberto, I want you to think carefully. What exactly happened the day she was killed? Where were you? Where were Lucas and Jimbo?" Grace felt heat travel through her veins and she suddenly remembered Benny's winter coat, the courage that begins to warm you after you put it on.

"I was painting the wood in the living room. Lucas and Jimbo were painting one of the bedrooms. Mrs. Macpherson was in her room." Alberto closed his eyes. "Lucas came out and said that Jimbo had an emergency with his mother. They had to go. I should stay and finish."

"Remember the time?"

"I think it was around three."

"And what exactly did Lucas do?"

"He apologized about some things he said about Lupe when we were having lunch."

"Then what?"

"Jimbo came out and went out the door. He didn't say anything. He always says, 'Hasta la vista, baby,' but this time he was preoccupied. Then Lucas went out carrying the red duffel bag with tools."

"Do they usually take the tools home?"

Alberto struggled to think. There was something like light in the questions Grace was asking, but his mind was too dark, too confused to see clearly. "Not until the job is done. We didn't finish. We had at least half a day of work left."

"Anything else? Anything at all about when Lucas and Jimbo left that you remember?"

This is such crap!

Alberto's brow wrinkled with thought. "I was on my knees painting the baseboard. Lucas grabbed my shoulder. Shook it a little, you know, to get my attention." Alberto's eyes opened. He said, excited, "That's how Mrs. Macpherson's blood got on my shirt!"

Grace held Alberto's hand. "You need to tell all this to the police."

"They need to search Lucas's house," Alberto added, his face brightening with discovery. "Lucas hit her, took her things, and she died later. She was dying when I left. I heard her trying to breathe. I could have helped her. I didn't."

"We need to insist they do an autopsy to determine exactly when Mrs. Macpherson was struck."

Get away from her!

"I remember something else now. Captain America told me to open the door to Mrs. Macpherson's bedroom and I obeyed him. I opened it."

"And then?"

"I don't know. I think I closed it, but I realized I had just done what the voice told me to do. That's how my fingerprints got on the door."

"Yes! You didn't kill Mrs. Macpherson. You see now?"

"But . . . we still have to prove it. I don't know if I can. My mind is . . . it is becoming harder to think. Someone is cutting off the power that makes my brain work. How can I prove I'm innocent when my thoughts don't fit together? When I say things that don't make sense?"

"We can go to the police together. I'll help you say what you want to say. I can be your voice if you need a voice."

"Why?"

"Why?" Grace looked away from Alberto's face for a moment. She felt the warmth in her heart and felt it travel throughout her body before she spoke. "I'm your friend. Friends help each other." After a few moments, Grace added, "Benny reminded me that being with you is what I should do."

"Our friendship creates too much risk for you." Alberto paused and gathered the courage to say what he needed to say. "I don't want you to be involved with me . . . anymore."

Grace kept her eyes fixed on Alberto's eyes. Grace thought that an hour ago, she had felt the same way. She could see in his moisture-filled eyes how much his words were hurting him. Did she hurt as much when she decided last night not to see him? But now, now she felt the hurt of not seeing him again. "You don't want me involved with you because . . ."

"The police will know you're helping me. You can't be with me anymore. They will give you a record. It will be very bad for the rest of your life."

"Is that the only reason you don't want me with you?"

Alberto tightened his jaw to keep any words from slipping out. He turned his gaze in the direction of a cardinal perched on the lowest branch of the tree next to them. Grace heard a car honking and when she turned to look, she saw a frail woman with a red scarf enter the church. The woman was carrying a vacuum cleaner with its hose wrapped around her neck.

"No, that's not the only reason," Alberto said, and then was quiet again.

"Alberto," Grace said, "we need to be honest with each other. I want us to be honest with each other."

"Something is happening to me. It's not just Captain America. It's like a darkness coming in."

"Alberto, please, there are doctors who can help you."

"Captain America is not out there. He's not a fantasma talking to me. Captain America, he's inside of me, in my brain. I am his ugliness. His evil comes from me. I'm not right. Already I've done things he commands, and it's getting worse. I'm damaged. How I hear the voice is changing over time. I'm believing in Captain America more like he's a real person now. A little while ago I was talking to him out loud like I'm talking to you now. There was a strength I had available to me and now it is leaving me. It could be that soon, I, me, whoever Alberto is, is not going to exist anymore."

"That's why you don't want to be with me? Because you're afraid you're not going to be you anymore?"

"Because . . ." Alberto stuttered. "I love you. I would rather not be with you than hurt you."

Alberto's words stunned Grace before she felt her heart expand. She was loved. She could feel Alberto's love envelop her. "That's love to you?" she managed to say.

"Yes."

"Kiss me," Grace said softly, fixing her eyes on Alberto's eyes.

"What?"

"I need you to kiss me."

Alberto leaned across the bench and made to kiss Grace on her forehead, but Grace lowered his face and kissed his lips. The kiss could have lasted five seconds or an hour. Grace didn't know. She kissed Alberto until his lips answered her question. They separated slowly, reluctantly, and then Alberto embraced Grace. He held on to Grace as if the wind would blow him away if he let go.

"Grace . . ." Alberto started to speak and then stopped. He could not find the words that needed to be said. It was good. It was good to have lived long enough to feel what he was feeling. He had found love in this life and that was no small thing. Alberto turned his face away from Grace and froze. A brown car and a police cruiser stopped in front of the church. There was a moment when the thought of surrendering to the police crossed his mind, but then Grace might get in trouble for helping him, and there was also the loud shouts of Captain America.

Run! You have only one good option! Take it! Now!

He tried to speak but there was a burning coal in his

throat and the only words that came out were: "I have to go now." Alberto stood and began to walk away.

"Alberto? Where you going?" Grace jumped up and ran after Alberto. She grabbed his arm. "Don't do this, please!"

Alberto pointed with his chin toward the church. Grace turned and saw Detective Lydell get out of the brown sedan and make her way up the steps toward the red doors.

Alberto placed his hand on Grace's cheek for a few moments. The silent message Grace received was both "I love you" and "goodbye."

Alberto pulled himself out of Grace's grasp. Somehow, he managed to cross the busy street even though his vision was blurred. He felt a force coming from Grace pull him back toward her. He ran and ran and ran.

Grace watched Alberto disappear down a side street. She went back to the bench and sat down. She hugged Alberto's backpack. After a long while she opened it. There was the picture of Alberto's family as well as two hundred dollars and a disposable phone. She found a slip of paper with a day, time, and address written on it. Then she took a deep breath and walked toward the church.

CHAPTER 21

G race was leaning on the hood of the brown car when Detective Lydell emerged from the church with the two uniformed police officers behind her. "Give us a second," Detective Lydell said to the officers. Then to Grace: "Where is he?"

"I don't know," Grace responded. "I thought he might show up here. I remembered after you left that he mentioned something about Jimbo's mother working in a church in Brownsville."

Detective Lydell shook her head, disgusted. "I'm getting really tired of the game you're playing. I'm about ready to haul your ass to the station and put you in a cell for forty-eight hours. I know one where the toilet's not working."

"It's not a game," Grace said calmly. "I'd like to find him before you do. I don't think you're going to treat him fairly."

Detective Lydell chuckled, amused. "Is that right?"

"I know you won't simply by looking at what you've done and not done so far."

Detective Lydell shouted at the police officers. "There's a coffee place down the block, guys. I'll meet you there in a few." She leaned on the hood next to Grace and said with sarcasm: "What have I not done, in your expert opinion?"

"Did you search Lucas's house?"

"He has an alibi."

"You're right. If Mrs. Macpherson was killed *after* Lucas and Jimbo left her house. But what if she was hit at three and ended up dying two hours later? It's not an uncommon occurrence with blunt force trauma. You could have waited until an autopsy was done before you went after Alberto."

"We found the woman's blood on Bocel's clothes!"

"Where? Where was the blood?"

"What?"

"Alberto remembers Lucas touching his shoulder when Lucas was on his way out. Was the blood on Alberto's shoulder?"

Detective Lydell stared at Grace, a smirk on her face. But Grace also saw a moment of doubt. Grace had hit a nerve. She pressed on. "I'll take that as a yes. Don't you find that strange? The only blood on Alberto was on his sleeve? Did you check to see if there were any finger-prints in that blood? No? Who's playing games here? Are you after the truth or simply want to put some poor, undocumented Mexican kid in jail? Case solved."

Detective Lydell balled her fist as if trying to keep her hand from punching Grace. "What's Bocel to you anyway? Whatever it is you and he have, you gotta know it's not going to have a happy ending. Right? Even if he's innocent, he's in this country illegally. Best possible sce-nario, he ends up in a detention center for a few months before he gets shipped back to wherever he came from. Worst case scenario, he gets hurt or killed when we arrest him. He stole a Beretta from John Wayne's safe. Every NYPD cop is looking for him and they've been told he's armed and dangerous. The odds of him getting out of this alive are not good. If you want him to live, tell me where he is."

Where did the strength that filled her come from? Why had it waited to show up until now? Grace spoke calmly, with assurance. "Why don't you at least search Lucas's house? You know that's the right thing to do."

"And did Lucas steal John Wayne's money and gun too?" Detective Lydell asked sarcastically.

"Yes! I think he did. He's been providing drugs to Alberto's sister. He stole the money and the gun knowing Alberto would be blamed."

"Who told you that Lucas was providing drugs to Bocel's sister?"

"Alberto mentioned it . . ."

"Yeah, yeah, and you didn't remember until now. Look, whatever happens, when I fill out my report, I'll need to mention your involvement in keeping me from finding Bocel. I was serious the other day when I said this could be damaging to your future."

"I know. I accept that."

Detective Lydell nodded and then walked away in the direction of the coffee shop.

Grace felt the pumping of her heart. Acting courageously was a rush. Grace touched her lips. She could still feel Alberto's touch there. She looked across the street at the bench where they had sat. It looked so forlorn with its peeling paint and missing slabs of wood. She wished that she had been as forceful and direct with Alberto as she had somehow managed to be with Detective Lydell. She should have said, "I love you," those worn-out words, but still, was there any other way to say it? *I love you. I love you. I love you now. Let the future stay in the future.* That last gentle touch with his calloused hand, that could not be the last time they touched, could it? He was damaged. But she was damaged too. Whatever she did to help, it would be to save herself as much as him.

Grace ran up the steps to the church, opened one of the red doors, and entered. Mrs. Jasmine was vacuuming the center aisle with forceful, rapid movements as if she were trying to remove stains from the blue carpet that only she could see. Grace stood on her path and waited for Mrs. Jasmine to look up. When she didn't, Grace pulled on a yellow extension cord connecting the vacuum cleaner to an outlet on the side of the church.

"Can I talk to you for a minute? I'm looking for your son, Jimbo."

"James's not here." Mrs. Jasmine looked toward the front doors as if trying to gauge how far she had to run to escape.

"I'm a friend of Alberto Bocel. He works with James."

"I know who Alberto is," Mrs. Jasmine said, looking suspiciously at Grace.

"Then you know he didn't kill Mrs. Macpherson. I'm going to prove that Alberto didn't do it. When I do that, the police will come after James."

Mrs. Jasmine sat on a pew. She looked tired, too tired to pretend. Grace sat in the pew in front of her and faced her. "James is not here. Not in Brooklyn. Not in the US. He gone. He didn't kill nobody."

"Then who?"

Mrs. Jasmine lowered her eyes, clasped her hands. "I don't know who killed that poor lady. Maybe your boy. Maybe Lucas. All I know, James didn't do it. He came home and said something bad happened at work. He had to leave. My son is good. A good person. He knows he be blamed sooner or later. Black man in the end gets all the blame. He left."

"Alberto is a good person too. He's getting accused of something he didn't do."

"I knows Alberto is a good boy, James told me. But good people kill too."

"James would help Alberto if he could. You know he would. James was the only person Alberto sought for help."

Mrs. Jasmine unwrapped the scarf from her head and used it to wipe the perspiration from her forehead and neck. "This Lucas, he is evil." Mrs. Jasmine crossed herself. "Even James is afraid of him."

"Is there anything you can give me? Anything that will help Alberto?"

Mrs. Jasmine shook her head vigorously. "No, no. You have to go." Mrs. Jasmine began to walk down the pew in the direction of the electrical outlet. She stopped halfway there and turned around. Without looking up at Grace, she said, "This Lucas, he liked to steal things from houses they painted. The painting job was an excuse to steal. My James would come home afraid he lose job. He said he'd tell Lucas not to steal but Lucas never listened to him." She paused. "James said Lucas bought drugs to sell. Lucas used drugs some but mostly he sold. Right out of his apartment. People knock on his door and buy junk from him. He wanted James to help him sell drugs here in Brownsville, but James said no." Mrs. Jasmine raised her head and pointed at the statue of a saint in the front of the church. "That there is Martín de Porres. There should be more Black saints like him."

"Do you know where Lucas lives?" Grace asked. "Please, this is important. Alberto is in danger."

Mrs. Jasmine made her way slowly to the altar. She reached behind the pulpit and opened a very big black purse. She lifted out a small spiral notebook. "James wrote addresses and phones in here." Mrs. Jasmine flipped through the pages. "Here." She tore a page and handed it to Grace. "Be careful. This Lucas is the devil himself. He will not hesitate to hurt you."

CHAPTER 22

Alberto moved fast. He had to get to Coney Island and prevent the CFE from cutting off the electricity to Rabbi Sacks's church. The CFE would no doubt soon find out about his love for Grace and they would move on to cut off the electricity to her building as well. The CFE could even shut off the power to Joseph's house. How would Benny play his music? That's how the CFE operated. If you were on their list, they cut off the electric current to your home and to the homes of your relatives and friends. Papá was the number one most wanted man on the CFE's list, and now they were coming after Alberto and his friends.

He found his way to Eastern Parkway, where a bus driver told him to go straight until he reached Kings Highway and then take Ocean Parkway to the end. It began to rain, and the bus driver offered to take him part of the way, but Alberto needed to keep his body moving and the cold rain muffled Captain America's voice. He had walked to Coney Island from Lupe's apartment many times before. It was a long walk, two hours at a fast pace, but he was not in any hurry today. All along Eastern Parkway there were families walking to church. Rabbi Sacks told him that Saturday was a day she dedicated to God. She would not do many of the work-like things she did on other days so her mind and body could rest with God. How would it feel to rest with God? Alberto imagined that rest to be a peaceful silence, like when baby Chato fell asleep in his arms, or when his hands slowly shaped a lump of clay into a bowl.

If Alberto could choose to live anywhere in the United States, he would choose to live with Joseph and Benny. But if he could live anywhere in the world, he would go back to Ticul. That's where he belonged. If there was any place where he could rest with God, that was it. And

Grace? Grace was from another world, not his world. He could see in her eyes and hear in her words that she felt something for him, but that was not enough to make a life together. Even he, uneducated as he was, knew that Grace's path in this life could not include him.

What was he thinking? His path in life was not going to be here or there. His path ended at Coney Island. The best thing he could do with his life was to make sure the CFE did not cut off the power to Rabbi Sacks's church or Grace's building or Joseph's house. He had reached a dead end. No way he could continue to live with Captain America inside his head. It was a short path, his life, but it would end in a good way. The tall CFE employee, he could not remember his name, would not visit Rabbi Sacks's church, and he would never find out where Grace or Joseph lived. It was a very small thing, making sure his friends never lost power, but wasn't life just one small thing after another?

As soon as Alberto noticed that the rain had stopped, Captain America spoke.

It's time for you to go!

"Will you ever go away?"

Hell no!

"I would like to be free . . . of you."

It's not possible.

"I can choose not to obey you."

You're doing exactly what I want.

Alberto started to cross a street, when a man in a purple van honked at Alberto. "Watch where you're going, pendejo!"

Alberto stepped back on the sidewalk and waved for the man to drive on. It was unbelievable that no one in Mexico had ever called him a pendejo. He had to come to Brooklyn for that to happen. Some pendejos were just dumb. Other pendejos had a streak of meanness. The tall CFE employee he was going to meet at Coney Island was mean. He could tell by the way he whispered that he had never lost a fight. *Dennis!* The tall man's name came back to him. Dennis did not know it, but he was going to liberate him from Captain America.

Grace sat on the steps of the building across from where Lucas lived. She had formulated a plan based on what Alberto told her. If Lupe and Lucas weren't together, then she would talk to Lupe and get information that would help Alberto. *She is family,* Alberto had said. Grace was hoping that blood would win over addiction, even if Lupe had betrayed Alberto before.

Alberto mentioned that Lupe and Chatito got into Lucas's yellow Toyota. There was no yellow Toyota parked on the block and there were lots of empty spaces for a car to park. Still, Grace had to make sure Lupe was alone. She had finally decided to sit on those steps because a girl about her age was already on the top step. The girl was smoking a cigarette and listening to a song with a very loud bass on her earbuds. Grace took a deep breath, waited a few moments to make sure her fear was well hidden, and then stood and walked up to where the girl was sitting. The girl glanced at Grace, annoyed. Grace motioned to her to take off her earbuds.

"What?" the girl asked. There was more suspicion than anger in her voice.

Grace dug into Alberto's backpack and took out one of the hundred-dollar bills she had found there. "Would you like to make a little money?"

The girl ignored the bill in Grace's hand and scanned Grace from head to toe. "Who are you?"

"I'm trying to help a friend who's in trouble with the police, but I don't think I can do it by myself. As you can see, I'm out of place here."

"You think?"

"My name is Grace. What's yours?"

The girl lit a cigarette. "Yvonne," she finally said, blowing out smoke through the side of her mouth. "What kind of trouble?"

"They think he killed a woman and then robbed her. He's undocumented, from Mexico, and is having mental problems."

"And you're the little white angel come down from heaven to save the poor Mexican boy."

Grace sat on the step next to Yvonne. "I . . . no," Grace said, thinking, her eyes fixed on the building across the street. "I'm here because I love Alberto. That's the boy's name."

Yvonne grinned a *been there done that* kind of grin. "What you want from me?"

"There's a guy that lives in that building." Grace pointed at a four-story dilapidated, brick building. "I need to make sure he's not home. But the woman he's with has a baby, so maybe she's there and I can talk to her. I looked all down the street and the next and couldn't find the guy's car."

"What's the guy's name?"

"Lucas. I don't know whether that's his first name or last."

"Lucky. Everyone around here calls him that."

"So you know him?"

"Who doesn't? He supplies the junkies on this street. He's not home now. I saw him leave just before you showed up. What you need?"

"I needed someone to knock on the door in case he was home. I'll be okay now, thanks."

Yvonne laughed and coughed. She stepped on the cigarette stub with her red sneaker. "Here, give me that. No one's gonna open a door for you." Yvonne snatched the hundred-dollar bill from Grace's hand, stood, and stuck it in the back pocket of her jeans. She wrapped the earbuds around her phone and climbed down the steps. She turned to look at Grace when she was at the bottom. "Well, come on. You want in? I'll get you in."

Grace followed Yvonne to the front of Lucas's building, where three teenagers were sitting on the steps passing around a bottle in a paper bag. Yvonne said something to them, and they all laughed.

The building was dark. It smelled like milk gone bad. Someone had taken a black marker and written "never worked" on the elevator doors. Yvonne and Grace took the stairs up to the second floor. They stepped out of the stairway and walked to apartment 2C. Grace closed her hands to keep them from shaking. Why was she so nervous? Lupe was a mother; how scary could she be? She needed a few moments to calm herself, but before Grace could say anything, Yvonne banged on the door.

"What are you doing?" Grace asked.

"I'm getting you in." Yvonne knocked again. From inside the apartment a baby cried.

"Lucas not here." The woman's voice sounded weak. "Come back later."

"I'm just dropping off some cash I owe him." They heard the rattle of the door chain.

The door opened a crack and a face peered out. Lupe's face looked haggard; her eyes were like those of someone emerging from deep sleep. When she was finally able to focus on Yvonne and then Grace, Lupe said: "I'll take the money."

"It's a lot of money," Yvonne said. "You need to let me in so you can sign a receipt." Lupe looked at Grace as if trying to remember where they had met before.

Lupe unhooked the chain latch and opened the door.

"You're in," Yvonne whispered to Grace, and left.

"Where she going?" Lupe asked.

"She has an errand."

"You can leave the money there." Lupe pointed to a table filled with cereal boxes and dirty paper plates.

A baby cried, and both Lupe and Grace turned their heads to a baby on a rug surrounded by pillows. Lupe went to get the baby while Grace scanned the room. Through the open bedroom door, Grace saw a night table with a small bag filled with white powder. When Lupe returned with baby Chato in her arms, Grace had taken a deep breath and steeled herself.

"Alberto is in trouble. He needs your help."

Lupe grabbed a baby bottle and filled it from a carton of milk in the refrigerator. She pulled out a chair and began to feed baby Chato. "Who are you?"

"I'm a friend who's helping Alberto prove his innocence."

"The police have proof. They told me." Lupe refused to look at Grace.

Grace sat on the edge of a chair. "And you believed them? How well do you know your brother?"

Lupe's eyes flickered with anger. "Get out!"

Grace felt the door she had begun to open suddenly close. She could not think of anything to say or do that would get her to say something helpful. Finally, desperate, she said, "Alberto hears a voice, did you know that?"

Lupe glared at Grace. "Just leave."

"His mind is not working right. You must have noticed something. Don't you care?"

"What do you want from me?" Lupe shouted.

There, there was the opening Grace was looking for. "You can tell the police who killed the old woman."

A look of recognition flashed on Lupe's face. "I thought Alberto . . . the police have proof he did it."

"The police are not investigating the other people who also had an opportunity to kill her. People like Lucas."

"Lucas?" Lupe laughed. "Lucas? You think Lucas did it? For your information, I was with Wayne when his aunt called him asking for help. Lucas had already left." Lupe turned toward the door when she heard voices on the hallway. "You better leave."

"Alberto told me about Wayne's money and gun, about his secret hiding place where he found a small amount of money. Someone else hid that money, didn't they? I think you know very well who it was."

Lupe's face turned red. The arm holding the bottle trembled. "You should go."

"Just give me something, anything that will help Alberto. The police think Alberto has Wayne's gun. They won't hesitate to shoot when they find him."

Lupe placed baby Chato on her shoulder and began to pat his back. "Do you know where he is? How is he?"

"No. He's running. Hiding. He thinks he's responsible."

Lupe bit her lips and then tears began to flow. "I . . . I thought Alberto killed the woman and . . . I needed the money to leave Wayne." Lupe turned her arm so that Grace could see a purple bruise. "Lucas said the money could set him up in business. We could be together. Wayne was hurting me. He kicked me and Chato out of the apartment."

Grace said, "Alberto told me Wayne was not good to you. But going from jerk to drug dealer is not a good move."

"You better go. He's coming back soon. He shouldn't find you here."

"Okay. I'll leave. But . . . Lupe, please, those tears tell me you love Alberto. You are the only one that can save him now."

"Lucas . . . I . . . don't have anyone else," Lupe muttered through sobs.

"You have Alberto. He's your family. And I will do all I can to help you and your baby."

Lupe shook her head and hugged Chatito to her chest.

Grace waited for Lupe to look at her. She stood and went to the door. There she turned and pleaded one last time. "Have you seen anything that may have been taken from the old woman?" Lupe shook her head. "Where would he hide something?"

Lupe was silent, thinking. "He hides the drugs in the laundry room downstairs. I just see him go up and down. One time he had one of those wrinkle-free sheets stuck to his shoe. He doesn't want his stuff in the apartment when he's not here in case someone breaks in."

"Thank you." Grace stood.

Lupe spoke just as Grace opened the door. "What will happen to me and my baby if it turns out that Lucas killed the old woman?"

"You'll get the help you need. I promise."

"Can you call me? Let me know about Alberto. I don't even know your name."

"My name is Grace." Grace took out her cell phone and tapped the number that Lupe called out to her.

"Grace, if you see Alberto, tell him I didn't have a choice. I'm still a good mother. I didn't have a choice."

Grace was suddenly filled with sorrow. Lupe's life, unlike her own, was not one that was filled with choices.

CHAPTER 23

Alberto walked slowly on the sidewalk adjoining the Ocean Parkway service road. On this block there were houses with front yards and driveways that led to one-car garages. A girl jumping rope reminded Alberto of Lupe. When did she start to get lost? A person doesn't take a wrong path all at once but step by step. Lupe's first step in the wrong direction was when she was fifteen. How did it happen that life in Ticul became too small, too confining for Lupe? The day the family went to the fair, when the picture Alberto treasured was taken, Lupe got into a fight with their father over her drinking and the company she was keeping. She stormed out of the house. What made Lupe different from Mercedes or Chela or him? No one else had her restlessness, her inability to be content. Ticul was never good enough for Lupe.

At least she has ambition.

"I have ambition. Taking care of my family. Working so Mercedes and Chela can go to school. Helping Lupe with baby Chato. Reading my high school books. Isn't that ambition?"

The ambition of a slave.

"Not *your* slave!"

You're worthless.

Alberto told himself to stop arguing with Captain America. Abraham could win an argument with God, but he could never win one with Captain America. He had been standing on the sidewalk looking at the girl jumping rope and talking out loud, and now the girl's father had come out and was taking the girl inside the house.

"Get the hell out of here!" the father shouted at him from the door.

He scared people. Wherever he went, even if he never did anything that Captain America asked him to do, people would be afraid of him. And why wouldn't they? Wasn't he crazy? Alberto heard a police siren. He started to run.

Grace looked for Yvonne on the steps across from Lucas's apartment, but Yvonne was not there. The whole street was deserted except for someone smoking inside a car nearby. The sun was directly on Grace's eyes, so she did not immediately recognize the person who came out of the car and was walking toward her. Grace shielded her eyes and smiled. "Let me guess. You got all the paperwork done and are here to arrest me."

"Yeah, I wish." Detective Lydell spat and then flicked the cigarette away. "Get in the car. We need to talk."

The inside of Detective Lydell's car smelled like a mixture of cigarette smoke and pepperoni. Detective Lydell had just sat behind the wheel when they saw a yellow Toyota Corolla stop and back into a parking space across the street. "That there's the guy you're looking for—Terence Lucas." Detective Lydell pointed at the man who got out.

"I don't need him anymore. I talked to Alberto's sister. She's in Lucas's apartment with her baby." Grace watched Lucas go into the building. She could not imagine what Lupe saw in the man. "That guy even looks like a criminal," Grace said.

"He is a criminal, or was. He's done time for drug trafficking."

"And still he was not a suspect?" Grace raised her voice, frustrated.

"I'm only one person. I put my time and effort on the odds-on favorite. That'd be your boy."

"How did you know I was here?" Grace tried to open her window.

Detective Lydell started the car. "They don't open unless the car is on." When the window was lowered, Grace stuck her hand out. It had begun to rain again. "I watched you go in and talk to Mrs. Jasmine. After you left, I went in and she told me she had given you Lucas's address. I couldn't come right away. I had to check on some things."

"I no longer have any doubts about Alberto's innocence."

Detective Lydell started to take out a cigarette but dropped the pack when she saw Grace grimace. "I saw the medical examiner before coming here."

Grace waited for Detective Lydell to continue, but she was now busy unwrapping a stick of gum. She offered Grace a piece.

"No, thanks. What did he say?"

Detective Lydell took the gum out of her mouth and stuck it on a paper coffee cup. "I hate cinnamon. So, I asked the medical examiner if she could push Mrs. Macpherson's autopsy to the head of the line. That was a solid no. But we got to talking, and she says it's possible that the blunt force trauma to the head took place a couple of hours before she expired. She's going to look for that when she does the autopsy, says the autopsy will for sure show it, if that's what happened." Grace stared at Detective Lydell for a few moments. "What?"

"I'm just a little surprised."

"I also called forensics and asked them to check for any fingerprints on the sleeve of the shirt where we found Mrs. Macpherson's blood."

"Really, you did that?"

"I did the right thing. You may find it hard to believe, but that's what I've done for the nineteen years I've been at this job."

"Thank you. I don't know what to say."

"Yeah, well. I got one more year and then I'm out. I don't want any regrets bothering my conscience when I'm in my backyard drinking margaritas."

Grace thought she saw a glimmer of a smile on Detective Lydell's lips. "I have one more suggestion."

"Great. Now what?"

"Lupe told me Lucas hides his drug stash somewhere in the laundry room of his building. What if that's also where he hid the things he stole from Mrs. Macpherson? I think a thorough investigation requires that you check that out. Lupe has no reason to lie."

Detective Lydell rubbed her forehead furiously. "Damn it, girl! Why do you insist on complicating my life?"

"I'm not complicating it. I'm simplifying it. *And* making sure that you get a commendation for brilliant detective work. When all the evidence pointed at Alberto, you alone pursued the truth."

"All right, all right. No need to blow smoke up . . ."

"There was a bag with white powder in the bedroom."

"How big was the bag?"

"A baggie, like the ones for sandwiches. It was full."

Detective Lydell stepped outside, leaned on the driver's door, lit a cigarette, and talked into her cell phone. "Hi, Margie. This is Bertha Lydell. Good, thanks. Question: Do I need a warrant to search the laundry room of an apartment building or will permission by the super or owner be okay? Owner? Okay. Great. Oh, I may need a warrant to search an apartment. Yeah, I got a reliable tip the owner is selling drugs. Will you hang close by for the next couple of hours? Thanks." Detective Lydell motioned for Grace to come out of the car. When Grace stood next to her, she said, "So this is what's going to happen. I'm going to find the owner of that building and get the okay to search the laundry room. I'm going to call the officers you saw back at the church to come help me. If we find anything incriminating Lucas, we'll get a warrant for his apartment. If we don't find anything, I'll get a warrant based on the drugs you saw in there. I may need you to talk to the judge, so stay by your phone. Right now, I need you to scoot on out of here. Can you do that?"

"Yes. Can you call me and let me know what happened even if you don't need a warrant? Do you have my number?"

"Oh, I got your number all right!"

Grace looked at the drops of rain splattering on the windshield. It occurred to her that maybe, just maybe, she had done what Alberto would have done had he been able. Now all she had to do was find Alberto.

Alberto loved making traditional Ticul water jugs. They could be as big as three feet tall and could hold ten gallons of water. Even after Ticul got running water, the water jugs were still popular with residents, who used them as flower vases. It was challenging to work with so much clay and it took a long time before Alberto was able to get good at it. But no matter how careful he was, jugs would still crack inside the giant kiln. Alberto would put five jugs in the kiln, all of them made with the same care, and one of them would come out with a split running down its side. A damaged water jug was useless. It would not hold water. No one wanted them, not even as vases to hold flowering branches. They were considered dangerous. Alberto would take the cracked jugs out to the back and smash them inside a steel drum. People would come by, take the broken pieces, and mix them with cement to strengthen and decorate walls or fences.

Alberto thought about the water jugs as he watched the waves rise and dissolve angrily on the beach. When he was in Ticul, Alberto had spent hours trying to figure out why one jug broke and not the others. Had he done something different, some carelessness on his part? Was it the location of the jug inside the kiln? No. Sometimes a jug near the fire broke and sometimes one farther away. There was simply no explanation, no cause, for a jug cracking.

If only whatever pieces remained of him after Captain America took over could serve some use, provide strength or decoration. But the only use he could think of was that he would not be a burden to others. How had it come to this—that he could no longer find the thread that kept him living day by day? Captain America's words had seeped into his mind the way red dye seeps into clay. He did not matter, just as Captain America said. He was a dumbass. Alberto thought of Michael, Grace's boyfriend. He was smart like Grace. He had a quickness about him, a command about his words, a confidence. That's the kind of person Captain America liked. Michael belonged in this country, not like him. Grace needed someone who not only fit in but was superior. Together they could reach out and grab tomorrow.

The rapid rhythm of the waves, one after another, kept Captain America quiet. The rain did that as well, and so did the wind and the trees. But Captain America would be back sooner or later. Alberto felt Captain America's presence even when he didn't hear him. It made no difference whether Captain America spoke or not. Captain America's words had become Alberto's very own thoughts.

The day was too cloudy to see the sun set, but Alberto could feel the light of the day grow weaker. It was strange that we only notice light when it is going away or when it's gone. His father died trying to give electric power to a neighbor so she could have a light bulb or two in her shack. And he, Alberto Bocel, the light that was Alberto and no one else, was slowly extinguishing.

CHAPTER 24

It was dark when Detective Lydell called. Grace was sitting on the living room sofa with the lights turned off. Miriam had left a note that she had a late meeting.

"I was hoping you'd call. Tell me." Grace reached over and turned on the lamp next to her.

"I'll make it quick," Detective Lydell said. "We found heroin, money, gold coins, a silver candlestick behind one of the dryers. Inside a hole with a false vent. The dummy had a notebook with his name written on it. We found some more gold coins in the apartment. We arrested Lucas and Bocel's sister. The baby is with child services."

Grace sighed. She was responsible for separating mother and baby. "What will happen to Lupe?"

"We'll see. She's willing to talk. Could get a deal. Tell your boy he's in the clear. We'd still like to see him, get a statement."

"Detective Lydell, we need to find Alberto. He's . . . there's something I didn't tell you. Alberto hears a voice. He may be mentally ill. When I last saw him, he was . . . he didn't have much hope . . . I'm afraid of what he might do."

"I can leave the BOLO in place but take out the armed and dangerous piece. It's eight thirty on a Saturday night and I'm beat. I don't think I can do too much more right now."

Grace slowly repeated Detective Lydell's words. *"Eight thirty on a Saturday night.* Of course! Hold on a second, Detective, please." Grace ran to her bedroom, cell phone in her hand. Alberto's backpack was on her desk. She opened it and searched the bottom until she found the piece of paper. "I'd forgotten about something I'd found in Alberto's backpack. Let me read it to you: Saturday, nine p.m., Coney Island, look for the green light—a block from handball courts."

"That's where you think he is?"

"Today is Saturday and it's almost nine. Please, Detective, do you know where this place is? Can you send someone? I have a bad feeling about this."

"Okay, okay. I'll get a squad car and we'll go take a look. Shouldn't be too hard to find."

"Thank you."

"Listen, if we find him and I take him to the station . . . Well, it'd be better if I didn't . . . given his status in this country."

"Bring him here," Grace said. "Bring him here."

Alberto was asleep on one of the handball courts when he felt someone tap his shoulder. He opened his eyes and saw a face he had seen before, but Alberto could not remember where.

"You showed up," a tall man said, grinning. Alberto rose slowly. "Let's go over to the warehouse where the fights take place."

They entered through a door underneath a green light. Dozens of men and women with beer cans in their hands were standing in a circle, smoking and laughing. Alberto noticed that he was barefoot. He'd taken his shoes off when he was on the beach and must have forgotten to put them back on. Despite the cigarette smoke, Alberto could smell salt in the air. Dennis put his arm around Alberto's shoulder and led him past two women into the circle. "What's your name again, Roberto?"

"Captain America," Alberto said.

"Captain America? That's awesome! Everybody, he says his name is Captain America!" There were shouts and hoots and laughter. Someone shone a spotlight on Alberto's face. Alberto raised his hand to shield his eyes.

"Where you from, Captain America?" Dennis began to unbutton his shirt. There were crosses and words in a strange language all over Dennis's torso. "Where you from? I asked you."

"Flatbush," Alberto said. He began to take off his shirt as well. A few of the women whistled. He dropped the shirt on the floor and felt the pain in his ribs.

"Flatbush? I mean what are you? Puerto Rican? Dominican? Colombian? Mexican? What welfare, ass-licking country do you come from?"

"Captain America is American."

"When we're done here, you won't be able to pro-nounce America because you won't have any teeth." Dennis began to dance and throw jabs.

"This fight is until one of us is dead." Alberto glared at Dennis. It was not a question.

Dennis stopped, was silent for a moment. The people in the circle ceased their chatter. "You want to fight to the death? Whoa! You got more screws missing than I thought."

"If I fight, you and your people will not go to the church where I saw you. Never. You will leave their electric power alone and you will not interfere with the electric power to any of my friend's houses. The CFE will never go after them in any way. That's what I'm fighting for."

"Kill him, Dennis!" Alberto recognized the bald man he had picked up and tossed to the side but could not remember his name.

Dennis looked into Alberto's eyes and said, "That was the deal. We fight, we leave your friends alone. We won't cut their power."

"We fight to the end."

Alberto could feel Dennis studying him, considering. Finally, Dennis grinned. "If you're so hot to die, okay."

The people in the circle were talking loudly, shouting at Alberto. Some were in a line with dollar bills in their hands. Then the lights flickered and Dennis began to duck and weave. His movements reminded Alberto of a sleek jaguar. Alberto saw Dennis's confident grin. The man had no fear. Alberto was surprised by the admiration he felt for the man in front of him. Maybe it was envy. People like him were destined to be the boss. He saw Dennis's right hand coming at him as if in slow motion and then he felt it land on his cheek. The crowd cheered. Alberto staggered back but managed to stay on his feet. How many of those hits would be needed to extinguish Captain America? Alberto stood still, rubbing his cheek. He was amazed at how calm Dennis was. There was no anger in the man. He was performing for people who admired him, people who spoke his language. Dennis moved slowly and carefully as if to savor the pleasure of his fists striking Alberto's flesh. The next right hook that Dennis threw missed, and Alberto landed a solid hit to the liver. Dennis groaned and made a *not bad* gesture with his eyes and mouth.

Dennis raised his arms in the air as if signaling that victory was about to come and then rushed at Alberto with a fury of kicks and punches. The old pains became new pains as Dennis pummeled his jaw, ribs, groin. Then both were on the ground, with Dennis sitting on Alberto's chest, battering his face. Alberto reached Dennis's chin with an uppercut. There was a sound like coins rattling on a bowl and Dennis spat two bloody teeth. Just then, when Dennis's head came within reach, Alberto grabbed his ears and twisted them. Dennis kept hitting the side of Alberto's face. Alberto's eyes swelled shut, blood poured out his nose and mouth, but Alberto held on to Dennis's ears as if they were tiny life preservers keeping him from drowning.

That's when Alberto saw Captain America for the first time. He was far away, as if Alberto were looking through the wrong end of a telescope. Then Captain America came closer, and Alberto could see that his eyes were bulging out and one of his ears had detached from his face. For the first time since the fight started, Alberto was filled with uncontainable rage. He let go of the dangling ear and gripped Captain America's throat, harder, tighter, all the rage pouring out from his abdomen, chest, shoulder, arm, and out his right hand. He had not expected Captain America to ever plead with him to stop, but that's just what Captain America was doing. Wheezing and pleading. "Enough. Enough." Alberto only increased the power of his hold. He did not have to be good anymore, just like Captain America wanted. He was finally free.

Captain America's body began to sag. A tattooed arm

offered Captain America a knife with a silver eagle at the end of the handle. The melody from one of Benny's songs entered Alberto's mind and he began to hum it. He let go of Captain America's neck and spread his arms on the floor. He felt a bolt of fire enter his right shoulder. He felt the blade's tip on the soft part of flesh beneath his Adam's apple. He waited for it to enter his body, but the blade lifted, and when he followed Captain America's frightened eyes, he saw two policemen and a woman running at them with guns drawn, rushing at Captain America, all shouting words Alberto could not understand.

Grace was lying in bed with the lights off when her cell phone rang. It was Joseph.

"We have Alberto," he said. Grace heard sadness in Joseph's voice.

"Where is he?" Grace sat up.

"He's in Benny's room. He's safe. He's got a knife wound but it's not life-threatening—"

"What happened? How?"

"Detective Lydell found him in some warehouse in Coney Island. She told me you had asked her to bring Alberto over to your house, but she thought he'd be better off here. Your building has a doorman and cameras and she didn't want to be seen helping an undocumented fugitive. Alberto hasn't been officially cleared yet."

Grace closed her eyes and felt the lingering warmth of Alberto's love and her own new, tender love for him. "Can I see him?"

"It's best if you don't see him right now. The doctor treating him says the wounds will heal. A hospital would be better, but we'll play it safe. Detective Lydell told me what you did today. Good work, Grace."

"I still don't know how I did it."

"Grace, there's something else. He's going to be okay physically, but his mental condition . . . has weakened. He's confused. At times he seems to think he's Captain America and other times he thinks the man he was fighting was Captain America. One minute he's crying, the next he's laughing. This is hard to hear, but he's upset we didn't let him die. It could be just the blows he took to the head. Or it could be a psychological deterioration of some sort. When his body has healed, he'll need to heal his mind. We can help, but Alberto must want to be well. He'll need to recover the will to live."

"Yes," Grace said. Body first, then mind, then life. Her mind leapt to the future for a moment. She saw Alberto reading his high school equivalency books. He was at the Brooklyn Public Library and she was sitting next to him. She was reading also, but now and then she'd raise her eyes and gaze at him. They were together, Alberto and Grace, and it felt right.

"Bye, Grace. I'll call you tomorrow with an update."

"Benny? What are you doing in Ticul?"

"You're in my room. I'm going to be sleeping on the sofa. I brought you an MP3 player with the holy music you like."

"Is it a sin in your religion to want to die?"

"If it is then our greatest prophets have sinned. Moses, Elijah, they all wanted to die at times."

"And God let them live?"

"Yes. He had plans for them. He reminded them that they had tasks they needed to complete. Like you. You still have tasks."

"Tasks."

"Yes. When you get well, Joseph wants you to paint the house."

"The house? What color?"

"Joseph's blind, remember? He could care less what

color. Any color. You pick it. Here, let me put the earphones around you so you can hear the music."

"If you see Papá, tell him Doña Valeria wants to know if he can connect her house to the electric lines."

"Shh. Close your eyes now. This song is my number one favorite."

CHAPTER 25

Early on Sunday morning, Miriam drove Grace to Joseph's house. Grace had told Miriam all that had happened the day before, and now Miriam was unusually silent. Grace waited for the questions to come. And they did. Miriam parked half a block away from Joseph's house and turned to Grace.

"What a week, huh?" Miriam didn't wait for Grace to respond. "I know you're still processing everything. I just want to know what direction you're headed."

"I was up until two a.m. last night. My head was spinning with so much thinking. Finally, I got up and wrote the very few things I knew for sure. I can give you those."

"Please," Miriam said gratefully. "That will help."

Grace dug in her bag and took out a page torn from one of her school notebooks. She unfolded it and handed it to Miriam.

1. Be Alberto's friend.

2. Learn what it means to be a Jew.

3. Volunteer at a psychiatric ward this summer.

"Wow!" Miriam sighed. "Only three little things, but they're loaded."

"Each one has implications, true." Grace folded the paper and stuck it in the pocket of her jeans.

"I can see some of the implications," Miriam said, turning the steering wheel nervously. "Learning what it means to be a Jew implies contact with Joseph and Benny."

"Yes. They and others will help me learn about Judaism."

"Summer job in a psychiatric ward tells me you want to make sure medical school and psychiatry are still for you."

"Yes."

"And if they're not? What happens to Princeton?"

"I have no doubts about college. I'm just not certain which college. There some good ones nearby, you know."

"Yes. There are. Okay. Well . . . that's something, I guess." Miriam rubbed her forehead. She closed her eyes.

"We don't have to have this conversation now, Mom."

"No, no. I want to know. Let me have the whole shebang. And being a friend to Alberto means exactly what?"

"That one only means what it says. I don't know what the future will bring. I trust that we'll find out what is best for him and for me in time. Right now, in his condition, the best thing I can do is to be a friend. Simply a friend."

"Okay," Miriam said quietly.

"He could use your help as well."

"Me? How can I help?"

"With his sister Lupe and her little boy. She'll need rehab for her addiction, help with immigration, a safe place for her and her little boy."

"Okay. I think I know some people, but . . ."

"Alberto will have some money coming to him. His cell phone was ringing late last night and I answered it. A young man said he had sold a comic book that belonged to Alberto. He got eighty thousand dollars for it."

"I'm not worried about the money needed to help Alberto or his sister." Miriam paused to gather herself. "Grace, I think I will eventually be fine with numbers two and three on your list, but I must be honest with you, number one is a little scary for me. I'm frightened about what the future will bring with him. Is that bad? Alberto's mental illness scares me. His being undocumented scares me. Your attraction to him terrifies me."

"I know, Mom. I really understand. All those things are scary. For me too. But the more I got to know Alberto . . . the more the fear went away. Something happened. A kind of faith and trust in who he is opened inside of me."

"That's beautiful. Well, let's hope I can grow up to be like you. Although I don't see it happening anytime soon. And Michael?"

"Michael and I need to talk. I hope we can be friends and see where things go. I'm hoping he will be okay with me being friends with Alberto."

"Are you in love with Alberto?"

"Mom . . ."

"I just want to give you good relationship advice. I'm good at it, believe it or not."

"A week ago, all I could tell you for sure about love is that I knew it could end."

"And now?"

"So many people showed me what love is. There's your willingness to listen to my doubts, to respect my questioning, even though it scares you. There's Benny and Joseph, Ernestina and Rabbi Sacks, their unbreakable loyalty to each other and their response to the call to help others. There's Alberto and his readiness to give up his love for me for my sake."

Miriam looked straight ahead, silent, her hands on the top of the steering wheel. Finally, she said, "Wow. I don't think there's any relationship advice I can give you. I'm signing up for classes from you, young lady."

"Mom. I'm so lucky to have you." Grace placed her head on Miriam's shoulder.

"Well," Miriam said, smoothing Grace's hair, "maybe I do have this advice: Be honest with Michael about what you are feeling and don't postpone the inevitable."

Grace was quiet, thinking. She sighed. Then, changing

the subject: "You're welcome to join me on item number two. We can learn about Judaism together."

"Mmm. I do like the idea of royally pissing off your father. Let me think about that. Give me time."

"You got it. We'll give each other time."

They walked hand in hand to Joseph's house. Benny opened the door and Grace immediately hugged him. "You're a young man!" Grace said.

"Of course I am," Benny responded. Then, his eyes fixed on the floor: "You . . ."

Grace saw Benny struggling for words. She bent down to look into his eyes. "I only went looking for Alberto because you called me. I had already decided not to. I put on the coat of courage because you asked."

"It wasn't just me asking."

"I'm beginning to understand," Grace said. Then: "How is Alberto?"

"He's going to be okay," Benny answered confidently. "I just know he is. He's been asking about you."

Miriam saw Joseph sitting in his chair and went to him. Benny took Grace's hand and led her to his room. Coming out of Benny's room was a man with a white beard and crinkly eyes. He offered Grace his hand, and Grace shook it. "I'm Dr. Nachman. You must be Grace."

"How is he?"

"Physically? He will recover in a few days."

"And his mind?"

Dr. Nachman pulled Grace away from the closed door and into the middle of the hallway. "We'll see. Once his body recovers, I'll take him to Mount Sinai for some brain scans and other neurological tests. If there is no obvious physiological cause for the disturbance, Alberto will be placed in the hands of my good friend Emma Gorin, the best psychiatrist I know. She will know what to do. In the meantime, Rabbi Sacks will take care of his wounds. And as for his mind, he's with people that care for him; that's a good place to start the healing process."

Alberto was sitting up in bed, propped up with pillows; his eyes were closed. A few feet from his bed a small window was open, and Grace could hear a bird chirping. She pulled a wooden chair from a desk, sat in front of Alberto, and watched him. His face was so swollen it was almost unrecognizable. His cracked lips moved as if he were reciting a prayer.

He opened his eyes and saw Grace. He laughed, a joyful, quiet laugh. It was the first time in his life that a wish had come true. "Grace," he said, "you found me."

"I found you." Grace's eyes suddenly filled with tears. She spoke quickly. "I have lots of good news."

"I'm sorry," Alberto said softly.

"Why? Why are you sorry?"

Alberto tried to swallow. The bird outside his window was a toucan, he was sure of it. Toucans loved to perch on the high branches of the flamboyán. He hoped the bird would keep on singing for as long as Grace was there with him. The song kept the evil voice quiet. "I killed the lady Mac," he said. "I'm sorry."

"No, no. You didn't. Lucas killed her. There is no doubt about it. We can prove it."

"And the tall man from the CFE, I killed him too."

"You didn't kill anyone."

"I wanted to die."

"But you didn't die. And now you're going to fight to get well."

Alberto saw the MP3 player with Benny's holy music. There was a small opening, a clarity in his mind at the end of which shone a dim yellowish light. Alberto had to tell Grace what he needed to say before the opening closed and the light went out. "I found you, Grace. I came into this world to find you. I did all I could so you wouldn't lose power. How could you get out of prison if you lost power?"

"I found power. I didn't lose it. I'm no longer in prison." She let the tears rush down her cheek and over her lips.

"I want to live."

"I want you to live."

"The toucan stopped singing. I'm afraid. The voice. The CFE."

"I'm here. Benny and Joseph and Ernestina are here. Rabbi Sacks is here. We're an army. No one can hurt you now."

Grace took Alberto's hand and sat on the bed next to him. After a while, Alberto closed his eyes. Grace waited a few minutes and then whispered a few words into Alberto's injured ear.

AUTHOR'S NOTE

Auditory hallucinations can be caused by a variety of neurobiological and psychological factors, including schizophrenia. My own experience with them came during some of the most intense manic episodes of bipolar disorder. During those times, I fought, sometimes unsuccessfully, against false images of myself presented by the voice. I was fortunate enough to be surrounded by a loving family and a caring community that believed and reminded me I was a good, ordinary, unique person regardless of what the voice said. Because of them and because I have been able to access the right medical help, I can now live a meaningful, useful life despite my mental illness.

Unfortunately, the support and care I receive is not available to many who suffer from a mental illness like schizophrenia. Our world continues to see people suffering from schizophrenia as violent, even when years of research and experience show that most people with schizophrenia are not violent. Schizophrenia, a treatable illness, is exacerbated by poverty, homelessness, addiction, and, most of all, by our fear of the illness and our rejection of the mentally ill.

One of the things that happens when we meet someone who is manifesting symptoms of mental illness is that we lose sight of the person behind the symptoms. The person hearing voices becomes a potential menace to avoid or a set of unpleasant behaviors that need to be modified. The result is that, not seeing themselves valued in the eyes of others, the mentally ill can lose their sense of self-worth and, indeed, their very self.

In writing about a young man struggling with the onset of schizophrenia, I wanted to show his inner struggle to remain whole and, at the same time, portray someone who is much more than his symptoms. I wanted to write a story about how mental illness erodes the sense of our own worth and how we recover it when someone has faith in us. My hope is that Grace's growing appreciation of Alberto and her openness to help him will encourage us all to see the person behind the mental illness and to respond to the call for our involvement when it comes.

ACKNOWLEDGMENTS

This is the kind of novel that I could never write alone. I am grateful to: Amy Peck, archivist for the Prospect Park Alliance, for her advice about Prospect Park and Brooklyn; my dear author friends Tziporah Cohen (also a psychiatrist) and Elana K. Arnold for their careful reading of an early draft of the novel and their generous and insightful comments; and Dr. Tasha M. Brown and Michael Birnbaum, MD, for their feedback on the portrayal of the onset of schizophrenia in the book. Emily Seife, my editor, makes my books much better than they start out to be. I owe so much to Faye Bender, my agent and friend, who was with me for the first book and will be there for the last. This story of love and healing would not have been possible without the love and healing I receive, now going on forty-five years, from my wife, Jill Syverson-Stork.

MENTAL HEALTH AND CRISIS RESOURCES

Below are some of the places that can provide support and encouragement if you or someone you know is experiencing symptoms related to mental illness.

SUICIDE AND CRISIS LIFELINE

https://988lifeline.org
Call: 988
Text: 988

NATIONAL ALLIANCE ON MENTAL ILLNESS

www.nami.org
Help Line: 1-800-950-6264
Text: HelpLine to 62640

CRISIS TEXT LINE

www.crisistextline.org
Text: HOME to 741741

SCHIZOPHRENIA AND PSYCHOSIS ACTION ALLIANCE

www.sczaction.org
Help Line: 1-800-493-2094
Email: info@sczaction.org

THE TREVOR PROJECT

PROVIDES CRISIS INTERVENTION AND SUICIDE
PREVENTION TO LESBIAN, GAY, BISEXUAL, TRANSGENDER,
QUEER, AND QUESTIONING YOUNG PEOPLE UNDER 25

www.thetrevorproject.org
Help Line: 1-866-488-7386
Text: START to 678-678

NATIONAL INSTITUTE OF MENTAL HEALTH

https://www.nimh.nih.gov/health/find-help

SUBSTANCE ABUSE AND MENTAL HEALTH SERVICES ADMINISTRATION

https://www.samhsa.gov/find-treatment
Help Line: 1-800-662-4357